MY LAUGH–OUT–LOUD LIFE

MAYHEM MISSION

BURHANA ISLAM

Published by Knights Of

Knights Of Ltd, Registered Offices: 119 Marylebone Road, London, NW1 5PU

www.knightsof.media

First published 2021

001

Written by Burhana Islam

Text and cover copyright © Burhana Islam, 2021

Cover art by © Farah Kahndaker, 2021

All rights reserved

The moral right of the author and illustrator has been asserted

Set in Bembo std/ 12 pt

Typeset design by Marssaié Jordan

Typeset by Marssaié Jordan

Printed and bound in the UK

A CIP catalogue record for this book will be available from the British Library

ISBN: 9781913311148

2 4 6 8 10 9 7 5 3 1

MY LAUGH-OUT-LOUD LIFE

MAYHEM MISSION

BURHANA ISLAM

For my family,
May He always keep us close.

~~MY SUMMER HOLIDAY STORY~~
~~THE ADVENTURES OF YUSUF ALI KHAN~~
MY LAUGH-OUT-LOUD LIFE
By Yusuf Ali Khan (Age 9 and 3/4)

Miss Minchell, my brand-new Year 5 teacher (yes, that's right, you heard it here first: Year 5! I'm one of the big boys now) has told our class to write about our summer holidays and she gave us this booklet to do it. Yes, I know, teachers make us do this nearly every year and, normally, I'm the third-last person to fall for this kind of stuff. The second-last person would be my cousin, Aadam, and the last person would be my arch-nemesis, Bashir, but we NEVER talk about Bashir.

BUT (and this is a big, big **BUT**), Miss Minchell said, and these were her exact words (no word of a lie): "There MAY be a little prize for the best storyteller in our class."

Then she winked at me. **DIRECTLY AT ME**. Nobody else – just me. It couldn't be a coincidence that she sat me in the first row, right in front of her desk, so I knew this was her way of secretly communicating to me that she had a pair of special edition Black Panther gloves with battle sounds with my name on it. ~~T'Challa~~ Miss Minchell, I will NOT let you down.

So here it is, my summer holiday story AKA The Adventures of Yusuf Ali Khan AKA My Laugh-Out-Loud Life. Now, let me introduce you to the main characters in my story...

AMMA

AFFA

NANU

AADAM

ME

Yusuf (THAT'S ME):

• I'm 9 years old (and 3/4), which basically means I'm almost an adult.

• Even though I'm almost an adult, Amma says I'm still growing into my teeth.

• I wear glasses – Affa says I have square eyes from being on my tablet too much.

• You might recognise my name from the Penalty Points board, but Amma has made me change my ways. She can be very persuasive.

AMMA (my mum):

• When she's wearing her hijab, she can look like an angel – especially with that smile.

• At home, she looks wild. Sometimes I think her hair is secretly hiding horns.

• Usually seen carrying a slipper to throw at me (see: persuasive).

NANU (my grandma i.e. Amma's mum):

• LOVES ME TO BITS (just like she should).

• She has no teeth and is always sucking on gwa and fan (betel nuts and leaves) like it's oxygen. She's not wearing lipstick and she isn't a vampire (I hope). It's the fan juice that makes her mouth red!

• She always has a tasbeeh (prayer beads) around her neck.

AFFA (my sister):

• Her eyebrows are always wrinkled because Nanu always picks on her.

• She has TWO names (Tammy and Farhana), which is SUPER confusing. But because she's soooooo much OLDER than me, I have to call her Affa, anyway (it's a Bengali thing).

• Her head is quite big, probably because she's got a very big brain. I think that's why she has a fringe. (Nanu hates the fringe).

• She's engaged to be married this summer to Umar Bhai (gross).

The other important person in my story is Aadam, my favourite cousin (and I have hundreds of cousins to choose from so that makes him extra special).

AADAM (my favourite cousin):

- My best friend in the whole galaxy.
- Has the most amazing gadgets.
- Still growing into his ears.

Normally, Aadam goes to Bangladesh for WAY more than a month during the summer, so my holidays are usually BORRRRING. All I do is sleep, eat, play on my tablet and then press repeat to do it all over again. I know it sounds fun, but it's not, especially after six whole weeks! I'll never tell anyone else this, but it actually makes me feel even more excited to go back to school again. But SSSSHHHHHHHH, that's TOP secret. I'm already the 29th least-coolest person in my class (and there are only 30 people to choose from!). That would make me a whole lot uncooler if that's even possible.

But not anymore!

This year, my homework booklet won't be filled with things I've made up – even though I do work extra hard to make them not sound like white lies (astaghfirullah).

Amma makes me say this every time I do something bad like tell fibs. It means 'God forgive me'. I secretly hope He does, otherwise I'm in big trouble especially after this summer.

I definitely didn't go to Disneyland or America or get some kind of deadly flesh-eating disease. BUT (another HUGE BUT) this time I did get myself into some extra tricky business involving THE WORLD'S HOTTEST CHILLI PEPPER, the BROWNIEST, SLOPPIEST and RUNNIEST paste in the whole wide world and a really, really, REALLY expensive red dress.

And it all started with a big sister, a bigger wedding and the BIGGEST problem I've ever had.

CHAPTER ONE

"Yusuf, are you even listening to me?"

My sister, Affa, always sounds like she has a blocked nose, but she actually hasn't. That's just her voice. She quack-quack-quacks like Daffy Duck. It's hard to ignore her even if you DESPERATELY want to. And trust me, I've tried wayyyy too many times.

"I always listen." I said. (I do, but sometimes I just pretend not to because it can get me out of very sticky situations.)

We were in her bedroom, hiding from Amma and Nanu. Affa was on the bed and I was on the floor, playing with her keyring torch.

"Prove it. What did I say then?" She looked at me with her beady eyes.

I knew that would happen. Luckily, I was always prepared because of my supersonic memory powers.

You have to have supersonic memory powers to be a hafidh and memorise Qur'an.

I'm nowhere near finishing so don't ask me where I'm up to. Don't ask my mosque teacher either! (Seriously, don't!)

It helped that I had just written it down in my notes for my summer booklet (the one you're reading right now) too, even if I did look weird doing it.

"You said," I took a DEEEEEEEEEEEP breath, threw Affa back her keyring, and closed my eyes. Rubbing my temples, I pressed rewind in my head. Who was I kidding? I didn't need help. My supersonic memory skills haven't failed me yet.

I put on my best Daffy Duck voice and puffed out my chest: "Now that I'm leaving home, sweet brother of mine, YOU have to be the 'man of the house'. You get me? None of this silly 'I'm-going-to-be-lazy-guts-for-life'. No way. That ain't happening. That ends now. You, my friend, need to step up. You hear me? You need to be there and help Amma and Nanu. They're going to be very fragile right now and things are going to change. It's important that Amma knows that we're still here for her. We've worked too hard to make things go back to the way they used to be. Do you understand what I'm saying? Why are you writing? What on Earth are you doing? Yusuf, are you even listening to me?"

I forgot to breathe when I spoke so I had to do it fast. Affa laughed and I felt dizzy.

"You missed out what 'fragile' means." She threw her pillow at me, but because I was already lying on the floor, it helped that I could use it for my head. Affa has hard floors with just one white, hairy rug.

3

"TAMMMMMYYYYYYYYY!"

Nanu has THE LOUDEST voice in our house. She's like a fire alarm. Affa never let her call twice, or three times or even more like I do either. She's too much of a goody-two-shoes for that anyway.

"Got to go, kiddo." And with a quick spin like the Tasmanian Devil, Affa grabbed her scarf and disappeared through the door. "REMEMBER WHAT I SAID, YUSUF," she called back over her shoulder.

As if I would ever forget. Me, of all people! Did she even know who she was talking to? There was only one tiny, little problem though… I was 99.11% sure that I didn't know what 'A MAN OF THE HOUSE' was and I didn't want to look like a baby by asking her and Aadam later. That would be a job for Sheikh Google.

Sheikhs are like the ULTIMATE teachers. They're supposed to be really smart and full of information - just like Google.

I could do the first step and step up, but I was just too comfy on the floor to be disturbed right now. And, anyway, where would I even step up to? The roof? I was already on the top floor.

4

CHAPTER TWO

"YUSUF ALI KHAN! Your bedroom better be clean,"

Amma's the type of person who always jumps to conclusions and thinks the worst of me. I mean, she's rarely wrong, but it would be nice if she didn't do that once in a while. Know what I mean?

Amma always sounded like she had a huge megaphone to scream into when she was angry. "And if your smelly clothes are still on the floor, you watch what I do to you, fwa."

Fwa means 'boy' (usually one that isn't your family or someone you love)

UH OH.

Everyone in our house had a superpower and Amma's was my kryptonite. She knew how to make your head hurt, heart stop and your whole body freeze without actually dying. Sometimes I thought being dead would be less scary!

I scanned my room and quickly activated speed-mode, targeting all the things that Amma would probably kill me for. It took her exactly thirty-seven seconds to come upstairs so time was already running out.

The whole room was a tip. My P.E. socks from two weeks ago were beside the empty box of Jaffa Cakes and my money box on the floor. The socks were covered with a glass bowl so the stinky smell wouldn't spread. If you looked closely enough and didn't breathe, you could even see life forms. RED ALERT: Amma would NOT be happy.

Twenty-nine seconds.

Not only that, but my school uniform, mosque thobe and every one of the clothes that I had worn for the past week, including my underwear, had exploded onto the floor.

A 'thobe' is like a really long shirt that reaches your ankles. It's great because not only do you feel so free, but if you kick your leg high enough, you can almost do a back-flip.

It was like a washing machine-eating dinosaur had vomited in my room and left the evidence there for Amma to inspect.

Nineteen seconds.

My bed wasn't made, the pillows were on the floor, my bandages were tangled in the corners of the walls and I was a dead man walking. Forget being 'the man of the house' – in one minute, I'd be buried UNDER the house. Amma would definitely kill me and then bring me back to life to dig my own grave.

7

Ten seconds.

There was no other choice but to take the plunge. I had to protect myself at all costs. I took a deep breath, blocked my nose and, like lightning, wrapped myself with EVERY SINGLE stinky item in the room. In shaa Allah that would cushion the blows. I wasn't prepared to meet my Maker just yet.

Nanu tells me to say this when I want something to happen. It means 'If Allah wills'.

Three seconds.

The smell was DISGUSTING. I thought I'd pass out, be sick or, at the very least, suffocate, but I guess God didn't want to meet me yet either. Even though Amma had never used the slipper on me before, I knew it was only a matter of time.

Two seconds.

I could hear her footsteps on the other side of the door coming closer and CLOSER and CLOSER.

One second.

Where was Nanu? Only she could save me now!

0.5638492 seconds.

I closed my eyes and braced myself.

Death was on the other side of that door.

CHAPTER THREE

It was like all the air had been sucked out and I was an astronaut in space.

A DEAFENING SILENCE flooded the room and an Amma-like mutant hovered at the door, ready to pounce on its prey. (GULP)

For Amma, there were always five levels of angry:

1. Di-ne di-ne badh os (Day by day, you get worse)
2. Ami morle sinbe (When I die, you'll know)
3. My all-time favourite: Thuy manush na goru (Are you human or cow?)
4. No words, but a slipper or any other household object that can be used as a weapon
5. DEADLY SILENCE

This time was definitely a level five. I was so scared that I had to clench every part of my body – and I mean every part! This was a BAD time – if not THE WORST time – to need to pee. This was DEFINITELY a bad day to have had four Capri Suns. I crossed my legs tightly, knowing that Amma wouldn't budge. Instead I just watched her, shaking like a young meerkat outside in winter.

Suddenly, Amma did something I had NEVER in a million light years expected – something so weird, so strange and so frightening that I thought that maybe an alien really had taken over her body.

Amma's face grew into a huge tomato and she burst into tears. She threw herself at me and squeezed me so tightly that I was almost 99.68% sure that my pee would trickle out. I didn't know what was worse: angry Amma or alien Amma.

"Yusuf Ali Khan," she wailed, almost strangling me with her scarf. "You will never, ever, ever, EVER leave this house. Okay, footh?"

means 'precious, loving, amazing, brilliant, extraordinary son' – except this was not the right time!'

Wait. What?

NOOOOOOOOOOOOOOOOOOOOOOOO!

How did Amma just go and do a full 180 from 'fwa' to 'footh' in less than two minutes? And what did she mean I would never leave this house? Didn't she know I had BIG plans? Was this what Affa meant by the 'man of the house'? Was it somebody who was chained to the house? NO WAY. Not if I had anything to do with it.

Amma finally released me from her death grip.

"You are a good boy, but tidy this room," she said, stroking my hair. "And why do you smell like pee?"

Oh, no! PLEASE, GOD. PLEASE tell me I haven't wet my pants!

After Amma left the room, I quickly checked. All clear. FALSE ALARM. It was just my old, smelly underwear. PHEW!

Trying not to throw up, I pulled off the mouldy clothes and threw them on to the floor again. There was no time to tidy my room. This was URGENT. I needed to find out what Affa really meant by 'man of the house', I needed to make sure that Amma didn't have the wrong idea and expect me to stay inside forever, and, more importantly, I desperately needed to pee.

CHAPTER FOUR

Amma and Nanu always said that men:

- were lazy
- were smelly
- did nothing to help in the house (I'm already a pro at that!)
- never smiled – even in front of a camera
- always forget things (the shopping list, the bills and sometimes, they even forgot that they had a family)

If that was the entire list, then maybe grown-up men were secretly zombies after all. Did being the 'man of the house' secretly mean I had to turn into a zombie? Did that mean I no longer needed to take a bath? Cooooooooool.

At least I could get some good zombie practice in at night-time when Affa put my bandages on. The only hard thing on the list would be forgetting everything. I'd have to sacrifice my supersonic memory to do that, but maybe it was worth it for the greater good. On the bright side, if I did that, maybe I wouldn't be haunted by that unspeakable day of 22nd March, 2017 when Amma gave away my Playstation to her other sister's son in Bangladesh. We don't talk about that anymore.

But everyone knows that nanus and ammas weren't the best sources for information, so I couldn't just rely on them. It was time to ask an expert.

Sheikh Google said that a 'man of the house' was a 'male member of the home that had the most responsibility for making decisions and taking care of the family'. If that was true, I was in trouble. Making big decisions definitely wasn't one of my superpowers.

And neither was looking after people. If anything, I needed everyone to look after me! This 'man of the house' business was going to be trickier than I thought.

I did more research because I'm actually good at finding facts. (Once I even got two reward points for my 'Plastics and the Planet' homework.)

Here's what I learnt.

A 'MAN OF THE HOUSE' must:

- be strong at all times
- take care of all family members
- open letters and pay the house bills
- do his best to make sure nobody gets hurt
- make sure there's always food on the table
- know what's going on in the house
- bring home the ~~bacon~~ halal chicken
- be the first one up and the last one down
- pray regularly

I think Sheikh Google accidentally missed this one out, but Nanu says prayer is the most important thing in the whole world. I'll have to find the prayer mat Khala and Aadam got me otherwise I'll forget too. There are some things even supersonic memory powers can't help.

I began to think that maybe the internet wasn't as truthful as I first thought because Affa was a girl and she did everything the man does and loads more. Somebody needed to write to Google to change that. But if my research had taught me anything, it was this: being a 'man of the house' was definitely going to be a challenge and with a list as big as that, I don't think just being a zombie will cut it. Affa was right. I would have to step up.

Step one: use the stool in the kitchen to step up. That, at the very least, I could do.

CHAPTER FIVE

DAY ONE of OPERATION 'MAN OF THE HOUSE':

Okay, first thing's first: a 'man of the house' was supposed to 'be strong at all times'. But my muscles were only just a tiny bit bigger than the size of a chana dhaal lentil.

This meant that I needed a little more training. Like Affa's wedding, I needed to plan carefully and put lots of thought into it so it would work out.

Amazingly, when I went downstairs to prepare my thoughts, it was almost like Amma had read them already. Maybe she had a superpower that even I didn't know about.

"Yusuf, help your affa bring in the shopping. NOW. I need to go feed my baby khodus while the sun's out."

Khodus are long, green bottle-y vegetables and Amma seriously loves them. Sometimes I think she loves them even more than me.

17

I never really understood why Amma always speaks to me like I won't do what she says. I guess only God can explain that. Anyway, as Amma came through the door and pulled her headscarf off (she brought in absolutely NONE of the shopping by the way – except her precious plant food), I decided to test my skills and flex my new muscles.

Affa drives a Juke (or a 'joke' as I like to call it) and it was quite high so this was my chance to properly step up. After putting on Affa's heels (they were the tallest sandals I could find), I dragged the loose brick that sometimes lives under our purple, spiky bush and pushed it next to the car. Doing this with pointy dagger-heels was not easy. I repeat: it was NOT easy. It made balancing on a wobbly P.E. beam seem like a walk in the park.

Okay: this was it. This was the moment Affa and I had been waiting for.

I took a deep breath and reminded myself that I was ready for this. I was worthy to be chosen and I could do this. I was Yusuf Ali Khan: former troublemaker turned respectful man of the house. With great responsibility came great power – every great superhero knew that.

With another deep breath, I relaxed my back, lifted my right leg and placed it on the brick. BAD MOVE! BAD MOVE! Affa's daggers slipped straight through the hole, nearly toppling me backwards. When I finally got my balance back and stopped wobbling, I lifted my left leg and placed it more carefully on the brick this time.

There! I had done it. I had stepped up.

Just then, Affa swung past me with a HUGE dead fish. GROSS! Its frozen ugly head was peeping out of the paper bag and it was looking directly at me like I was the one who had caught it. Look here, fish-guts, it wasn't me who stole you from your underwater home and your other fishy friends, I swear. Just as we locked eyes, I slipped off the brick, but luckily, I grabbed three shopping bags on the way before I hit the ground with a little crack.

"I'm okay!" I yelled, picking up the carrier bags and jumping up. "I'm okay." See, even when I was clumsy, I was on top form. If carrying three bags of bread, biscuits, toilet tissue, kitchen roll and Jaffa Cakes (yes!) wasn't 'man of the house' material, I didn't know what was.

I stumbled into the house and out of Affa's pointy shoes, smacking right into Nanu and her walking stick. She was busy pressing her prayer beads and she did not look very pleased at all.

Something was wrong and somebody was going to pay for it. Please, God, don't let it be me.

CHAPTER SIX

My heart thumped loudly in my chest.

Nanu's eyes glittered.

For a split second, there was silence.

Then suddenly, in the squeakiest voice, Nanu beamed, "Oooooooh, such a good boy. Look at my big, strong Eesoof." She's never been able to say my name right. Honestly, she's worse than the people at school. Then Nanu snapped. "Tammy! Why is my grandson carrying in twelve whole bags of shopping on his own? Have you no shame? He's just a little boy!"

Affa came back in with her eyebrows wrinkled, carrying a huge box of washing powder that was nearly as tall as me. She gave Nanu a sloppy kiss on the forehead before answering - gross. "Your daughter told him to, Nanu. Not me," she said, rolling her eyes. "And it's two bags, not twelve."

"Three actually," I piped up. I'm sure 'a man of the house' had to be helpful too.

Affa stuck her tongue out at me. BAD TIMING because Nanu actually CAUGHT HER.

AHAHAHAHA. She ACTUALLY caught her! To celebrate Affa's mistake, I popped open the Jaffa cakes with my free fingers and tossed one in my mouth. **CHOMP CHOMP.**

"Farhana Begum!" Nanu shouted. Her voice shook the walls. (Affa has two names, remember? I don't understand either – it's a Bengali thing.) "Never, ever, EVER drag that tongue of yours out of your mouth like that ever again. God will cut it right off. How dare you? And calling your own mother 'my daughter'. HAVE YOU NO SHAME? You are about to become a married woman. What on Earth are you playing at? Do you want to be divorced before you even say 'qobul'?"

Qobul means 'I do or I accept'

I was dead. I knew it. Affa would kill me the moment Nanu left. I really wanted to burst out laughing. Instead, I did something worse. Much worse. I waited for Nanu to turn her back to me and stuck my tongue out at Affa. I don't know what made me brave enough to do it, but I did it. I really did it.

I shouldn't have done what I did next either, but Shaytaan got the better of me. I must have been on a power-rush because I said the words every brown kid hated to hear. Words that started wars in families and tore them apart. Or so Aadam had said,

"But Nanu, what will people say?" I asked, innocently. Okay, I have to confess, I was kind of scared when I said it. Who knows what kind of evil those words could unleash?

"You little—" Affa started, giving me the biggest daggers. Thank God Nanu was there to protect me.

"Young lady, I'll speak to you later. You and I need to start your 'How to be the Perfect Wife' training. You don't want a failed marriage, do you?" And with that, Nanu swept her sari straight into the kitchen and dove nose first into the cupboard for her beloved gwa fan. "Take your nana and me," she called. "Only death came between us."

"You're going to pay for that," Affa snarled, undoing her scarf like she was rolling up sleeves.

I didn't feel so safe now. Not out here on my own where there were no witnesses. "NANUUUUUU?"

"Yes, Eesoof?" She sounded so far away.

Affa smiled mischievously. "Yusuf just needs help. He's made a mess on his pants again."

"What?" I shouted. "No, I haven't!"

"Yes, Yusuf Ali Khan. You have."

I looked down. OH NO. In all the commotion, I didn't realise that the eggs had cracked and leaked all over me. Oh no, they must have broken when I fell. That's what that crack was!

"Here." Affa plopped the huge box of washing powder at my feet. "Take this upstairs, my big, strong brother."

This was definitely a bigger step than I had planned.

CHAPTER SEVEN

"And I couldn't even push the washing powder to step one, never mind all the way upstairs," I explained to Aadam, filling him in on the whole story. We were in the living room while Khala and the others folded samosas for Affa's Mehndi night in the kitchen. "It was a total disaster. If Rabia Affa and Nayma Affa and all of them lot hadn't come to help with the sweet boxes, I would have been toast. Burnt toast."

I gave Aadam another Jaffa cake and stuffed the eighth one in my mouth quickly before I had to speak again.

"Phew, good timing then, wasn't it?" he said. His sticky out hair bounced higher every time he spoke.

I watched Aadam eat the chocolate first, then the orange jelly and then the spongy bit. "I know, but now I'm back to the beginning. How am I going to be the 'man of the house' if I'm not even strong enough for the shopping? The man of the house has got to go to the shops almost every day!"

"My dad does it easy peasy." He zipped his jacket and then unzipped it again and again and again.

"Yeah, but he's had a million years of practice. I mean, come on, he was alive before WIFI existed. I don't have that much time. Affa gets married in less than 22 days and then everything will fall on me." I looked around the room to see if anybody was there. The other sofa was empty and nobody was in the space behind it. The doors were shut tight too so the coast was clear. The only thing staring at us was the picture of me I drew for my summer homework booklet. I drew myself so well that it was like a reflection watching us.

"I know Nanu loves me," I whispered, stabbing the imposter's eyes so I couldn't see his wild glare. "And I like her lots too, but she's always wanting something. Sometimes I hear Affa get up in the middle of the night just to give her a snack or to help her pray. Sometimes Affa even sleeps next to Nanu when Nanu gets scared and sees things that aren't really there. There's no way I can do that. I can barely wake up for school!"

Aadam sighed and stopped zipping. "You don't have to do ALL of that on the first day. Spiderman fell from so many high places when he first started, remember? But he practiced a lot, didn't he?"

As usual, Aadam was right. He might only be 136 days older than me, but he was 100% a wise, old egg. Spiderman flopped, bumped his head and bruised like a peach when he first got his powers, but soon enough, he was swinging from buildings to branches like Mowgli on a sugar rush.

"You can do it, Yusuf. I believe in you." Aadam squeezed my shoulder. "Just watch. You'll be way better than all the other men of the houses. I know you will." He stopped. "What are you doing?" He asked curiously, looking at my booklet.

"I'm writing it down in case I forget." Even though I won't, of course. I scribbled quickly with my pen (yes, that's right! No biggie. I already have my pen licence. I got it on 22nd June, 2018 in a Literacy lesson at the end of Year 3. I still like to remind the whole world about it sometimes).

"Why are you doing that?"

I could tell Aadam was a bit jealous. He doesn't have his licence yet because he still can't hold a pen properly. His fingers wobble all over the place when he writes his name.

"Miss Minchell told us that the better the summer booklet, the more reward points we'll get. I'm going to try and cash mine in for a Nike football this year."

Aadam's eyes began to bulge out of its sockets. "Can I be in it? Can I be in your story?"

"Obviously! Every hero needs a sidekick, don't they? We can be like Batman and Robin!"

"Wallace and Gromit?"

"No! More like Ant-Man and the Wasp."

"Wait, wait," Aadam said. "I got it! Phineas and Ferb, right?"

I nodded eagerly.

"Anyway, heroes don't give up either. None of them do." Aadam read over my shoulder. "You've missed out when I said 'I believe in you' by the way. Oh wait! I got a better one. Do 'anything is possible if you only believe'."

I quickly squiggled it down, but it looked like a chicken had scratched it instead of a human so I had to cross it out and do it again neater. I needed these notes later to write up the best ever summer holiday story.

"Done!"

At that very moment, my spidey senses tingled. Aadam's nostrils flared wide open too and sniffed the air. Amma and Khala must have finished because a waft of Jannah seeped into the living room.

Heaven

27

"CHICKEN SAMOSAS!" Aadam and I squealed together, jumping up. These weren't just any samosas, they were soft, fluffy, handmade, melt-in-your-mouth, doughy samosas. Once you have one (who am I kidding? It's impossible to stop at one!) the flaky ones just don't cut it anymore. We screamed so loud that I was sure even the neighbours would be able to hear us.

"Come on!" I opened the door and ran, reminding myself to leave at least one samosa. A 'man of the house' always left food on the table, after all. See? Things were looking up already.

UPDATE: So maybe I took a teeny weeny bite of the last one (it was SO YUMMY), but it's the thought that counts, right?

UPDATE TWO: I said this to Affa and she said, 'You can't eat thoughts!' and was mad again. (Oops.)

CHAPTER EIGHT

Once a week in the dead of night when the curtains are tightly shut and the clock strikes the hour of bedtime, Affa transforms into her alter-ego: a mad scientist. Her hair goes all wild and frazzled, her cheeks burn red and she cackles like a deep-fried samosa while she sniffs her weapon of choice: the bandages. After double checking the door is closed to trap us both in, Affa slathers white cream all over my back, my legs, my arms and my tummy. Then she wraps and wraps and wraps me up like a mummy (but a zombie sounds way cooler so a zombie it is). She's done this ever since I can remember and I've gone from being an actual real-life reptile zombie with no eyebrows to a human being who has something that sometimes looks like real skin.

It used to be worse, believe me. One time, Aadam stayed over and he thought I had devoured a cheese pasty as a midnight snack without him. The only way I could stop him from eating the little flakes was by admitting that he was actually eating me!

It sounds babyish, but this was mine and Affa's special time to pretend that we were dead and wreak havoc on the living peoples of this graveyard (AKA our house, AKA Amma and Nanu, AKA both of us were still too scared to scare them, so AKA just us).

But today was a dark day. Today Affa showed me her true colours. Today Affa BETRAYED me. And she did it like it was no big deal. But actually it was a MEGATRON BIG DEAL. Affa had gone to Tariq Bhai's new house because Bhai and Bhabi (his new wife - who I haven't EVEN MET by the way) were having a fancy pants, grown-up party for Affa's new life. And I wasn't invited. Yes, that's right: the most important person in her life hadn't been invited. What's worse is that I didn't even get to go to Bhai and Bhabi's wedding either. When I finally found out he was married, I had already missed out on the chance to eat my whole weight in bombay potatoes, tandoori wings and my favourite, mouth-firing chilli chops. To make up for it, I'd promised myself that I'd eat double at Affa's wedding. (There's really nothing like regretting food you never got to eat.)

But, right now, Affa wasn't here and I was on my own. Completely on my own.

Bandaging myself was a whole lot harder than it looked and took a whole LOT longer than expected. This is what I had to do:

1.   I had to pile a load of pillows and blankets, and boxes of games on top of each other just to get the tub of eczema cream. I guess somebody thought it would be funny to put it wayyyyy out of my reach.

2.   I had to touch the white stuff inside. (The cream was ALWAYS FREEEEEEEEZING COLD so it was like getting a high-five from Jack Frost, which is never, ever fun. Trust me.)

3.   Then I had to plaster the iciness all over my pasty parts while trying not to get new-moon-ia and die. I could barely BBBBBBRRRRRRRing myself to do it.

UPDATE: Affa says this is actually spelt 'pneumonia', which just doesn't seem right to me.

4.   One of the hardest parts was reaching for my back. I basically had to HUG myself SUPER tight – but I quickly gave up when I remembered that I wasn't an octopus and couldn't do everything.

5.   I had to quickly put the bandages on before I became a human ice lolly and before the cream went all over the carpet, the bed, the walls and all the smelly clothes. (Okay, so I wasn't so good at that

bit, but neither was Affa really. If you looked closely on the floor, you could see an old dent from the one time I just slipped out of Affa's hands).

6.   The last step was to move all the little bits of furniture around the room so the place looked tidier.

Then TA-DAH! Zombie Yusuf Ali Khan is at your service!

Normally, when Affa's finished, I'm all bed-ready. But this time, when I looked around, I couldn't even see my bed. It had to be underneath all of this mess somewhere, didn't it? At least I knew one thing for sure – I didn't really need Affa anymore. My way of doing things was way more fun.

OUCH!

Well, okay, it was more fun until the box of board games came crashing down on to my foot.

CHAPTER NINE

Yes, Summer Holiday Story, I was still here over a thousand seconds later (that's MORE THAN fifteen minutes, by the way) and I was growing bored. I was all finished creeping around the room, moaning and groaning like the shivering undead, but nobody was here to listen.

If Affa was here, she'd usually pretend to die a painful death after I imaginary ripped her arms off, which was actually really funny (DON'T TRY THIS AT HOME). She'd fall to the floor and shout 'I TRUSTED YOU! I TRUSTED YOU! I TRUSTED YOU, BUT YOU BETRAYED ME!

'YOU'   *choke, cough choke*
'YOU'   *choke, choke, cough*
'YOU KILLED'   *cough, cough, choke*
'ME'   *dies*
'I'm dead.'   *dies again*

And then the police inspector (me) would tape the crime scene with the leftover bandages and cover her pretend corpse with a blanket. We always ended up rolling around on the floor and laughing so hard that I had to use my inhaler and Affa needed to go pee.

"I don't need Affa to have fun," I told myself. "I don't need anybody except me."

I could prove it too. Grabbing my bandages and rolling them across the floor, I tried to make the shape of a corpse. I dipped my fingers into the tub and drew a sad face on the floor where the face would be.

Then I got into character. After taking a deeeeeeeeeep breath, I focused carefully. I could do this. I knew I could.

I tried to drop to my knees, but the bandages made it pretty hard. Closing my eyes, I took a deeeeeeep breath.

"AHHHHHHHHHHHHHHH," I wailed, slamming my fists on the floor. "Why did you have to go? WHY DID YOU HAVE TO LEAVE ME ALL ALONE? WHY, OH WHY, OH WHY? AAAAAHHHHHHHHHHHH—" Make no mistake, I was definitely talking about the imaginary dead body on the floor. No way was I thinking about Affa. No way at all.

"Yusuf?" Amma interrupted. Her voice was coming from downstairs.

I looked around quickly. Meerkat mode had been turned on: this room, that bed, me! This whole place should be quarantined. If Amma came upstairs, she'd kill me. Zombie Ali Khan would be no more. I was a dead man walking. To make it worse, I was sure that real people didn't rise from the dead so soon either!

"Are you okay, baba?" she asked. Her door creaked. She must still be in her bedroom.

Act normal, act normal, act normal. "Ji, Ammu-jan? Yes, I'm just fantastic, thank you." I held my breath.

She still hadn't closed her door. "You go to sleep, Ammu-jan, okay? Everything's okay up here."

Curse my brilliant acting skills! If I wasn't careful, they'd get me into some serious trouble.

"Okay, baba," she called. "You go to bed too."

And with that, her door clicked shut quietly.

PHEW! That was close. I turned back to the pretendy-dead-body, which looked more like a potato smiley, and kicked it to the corner of the room.

You know, if I was forced to tell the truth, I might say that it just wasn't the same without Affa here. It just didn't feel right. Maybe this was how it felt to be a real zombie. It was like having a whole belly of emptiness.

I really was left with no other choice but to wake Nanu up and scare the heebie jeebies out of her. It wasn't like I could do it to Amma. She'd scare the heebie jeebies out of me. Even without bandages.

CHAPTER TEN

PLIP-PLOP.

That, my friend, was the sound of our letterbox AND the beginning of a new dawn for Yusuf Ali Khan, the man of the house.

I might never have opened a letter before, but that was only because I didn't get any. The ones we got were usually for Affa, Amma or Nanu, and I always found them in the bin about ten seconds later.

Anyway, because today was ATTEMPT TWO of OPERATION MAN OF THE HOUSE, things were changing around here. There was a new cowboy in town and he had V. I. B. (Very Important Business) to do.

Slowly, I came down the stairs, cracking my knuckles to get them ready. This 'man of the house' had letters to open. Not just any letters: very important letters. I'll be honest, I had to stop the knuckle thing pretty quickly because it started hurting a little. Oh man!

Today, we had six envelopes: one for Nanu (something about her eyes maybe?), three for Affa (she always got the most), none for Amma, and one for the 'Owner'.

Affa said that it was against the law to open somebody else's letters. Knowing her, she wouldn't think twice about sending me down, so I had to be careful. That meant I could only look at the last one. I ripped it open and, instead of being an ordinary white letter, this one was bright red.

With huge words, it read:

DEAR OWNER,
You have an outstanding bill of £1287.38. If the payment is not made immediately, legal action will be taken. Your house may be at risk of repossession. PAY NOW or lose later!

HOLD ON ONE SMELLY MINUTE. £1287.38! How on the whole of planet Earth, the sun, the stars and the galaxies beyond was I going to pay that? Who in the world was 'The Short Term Loan Company'? And, most importantly, why did they want to take our house?

I ran upstairs with my heart thumping. Sweat was trickling down my armpits already and flapping upstairs didn't help. I was sure my glasses would steam up from the smoke I imagined was coming out of my ears. Before the smoke could cause lasting damage, I scanned my room like a hawk.

There it was, right in the corner of the room beside the mouldy P.E. socks and the now two empty Jaffa Cakes boxes: my life savings. I quickly pulled off the lid and spilled the money on to the floor.

Before my very eyes was thirty-eight weeks of hard earned smackeroonies. I had already lost count of the amount of times I had to pretend I didn't want the money random aunties gave me.

£87.21 and £700 in monopoly money that I could cash in later – that was all I had. That meant I would need another … £500.17! (I'm a mental maths king, by the way.) It would take me light years to save all of that! Even if I sold Affa's laptop and phone (Affa owns an iPhone that's even older than me!), I still wouldn't have enough. It was impossible. We were doomed. I was 103% sure of it.

CHAPTER ELEVEN

It was official: my 'man of the house' days were over. I knew Aadam would be disappointed in me and say that Spiderman didn't give up after the first try. But at least he got some help from a super spider. All heroes had help, and anyone who said they didn't was lying. Superman had the sun, Ant-Man had the Pym Particles, Wolverine had Adamantium claws – even Thanos had the Infinity Stones to help him with his evil plan!

And then there was me. Plain, old, handsome Yusuf Ali Khan.

What chance did I have? It wasn't like my super smelly socks had radioactive powers, did they?

I left the red letter under Affa's door then put my life savings back into the money box, and in its rightful place next to the Jaffa Cake boxes.

With less than twenty days to go until Affa's wedding, I needed another plan. But my brain had been emptied of its juices and the only thing I could concentrate on was the quiet **TICK-TOCK** of the clock:

TICK-TOCK, TICK-TOCK, TICK-TOCK.

It almost sounded like my heart.

THUMP, THUMP, THUMP, THUMP, THUMP, pause, Oh no, it stopped! **THUMP**. Oh wait, no it hasn't. Phew!

"What are you thinking about, my kholja tookra?"

means 'piece of my liver'

"AAAAAAAAAAHHHHHHHHHH!

Nanu!?" I screamed, jumping to my feet. Forget the ticking clock, my heart was zooming like a race car on fire. "When did you get here?"

Nanu scratched her head and lifted her feet onto my bed. "It was the long winter of 1973 after the old war between East Pakistan and—"

"Nanu! I mean my room. When did you first come into my room?"

"Well, your Abbu bought this house before he—"

"Nanu, today!" I groaned. "When did you come into my room here today?"

"Oh, why didn't you just ask?" She was pressing her prayer beads again. "Only five minutes before you ran in here crying."

"I wasn't crying!" I swear I wasn't. Sometimes I get a little bit of hayfever in the summer.

"It's okay. You don't have to hide these things from your nanu. Grown men cry all the time. The amount of times I made your…" She trailed off. "Anyway, what's the matter, beta? Your shoulders look heavy."

"They're not. I'm just being lazy, Nanu." I starfished on the floor, trying not to focus on Nanu's toenails. They were tough and almost black. Once, Affa had to get a pair of pliers to cut the big toenail on her foot because the clipper got stuck in it and broke. The nail went flying into the air and nearly knocked me clean out. I actually had to nosedive just to dodge it. Even now, nobody knows where it went. Something tells me it's still hiding in the carpet somewhere, waiting to take its revenge.

"Cheer up, my Eesoof and give your nanu a lovely foot massage."

I froze, trying not to think anything. Nothing. Especially not her cracked up, razor sharp ninja feet. Was it possible that Nanu could read my thoughts too? Did I think that out loud? Did she notice? Affa had told me that Nanu had feelings and I definitely didn't want to hurt them.

Nanu ignored me. Maybe if I didn't look her directly in the eye, she'd forget she asked.

"This room's a mess," she said. "How is your sister going to manage a marriage if she can't even clean her brother's room? Tut, tut, tut."

It was then that it came to me: my light bulb moment. It hit me like a life-size Jaffa Cake. I couldn't believe that I hadn't thought of it before. Maybe Affa, in the end, had the wrong idea after all. Maybe this 'man of the house' business needed a different approach...

CHAPTER TWELVE

~~OPERATION MAN OF THE HOUSE~~

DAY ONE OF OPERATION STOP THE WEDDING.

Okay, you might think that I was taking it too far, but I wasn't. Trust me. Some things just needed to be done for the greater good and this was one of them. When Affa told me that it was my turn to be the man of the house, she was wrong. It wasn't the man-of-the-house's shoes that needed to be filled. It was the Affa-of-the-house's shoes.

And let me tell you straight: there was no way on planet Earth, the sun, the stars and the galaxies beyond that I'd ever take on that job. No way. The only choice we had as a family was to stop her from leaving. I mean, who did she think she was, being so selfish and only thinking about herself? Nanu definitely didn't raise her like that, so somebody needed to step in – that was where I came in. Yusuf Ali Khan, the hero. Sometimes you really just have to take one for the team.

Now that OPERATION STOP THE WEDDING was all systems GO GO GO, I had to put on somebody else's shoes and think about how I'd even pull this off..

I actually thought of putting Nanu's sandals on because they were almost the same size as mine, but then I thought really carefully. All this time I had been thinking about Spiderman when I should have been more realistic, more serious and … more grown up. Of course! Batman!

If Batman was in my shoes, what would he do? Like me, Bruce Wayne doesn't really have superpowers. Everything was in his head. In fact, the more I thought about it, the more I realised we had a LOT in common.

~~Me~~ Batman	Me ~~Batman~~
Super-smart brain skills	Supersonic memory skills
Has to protect Gotham	Have to protect my house
Can't tell anyone what he's up to	Can't tell anyone what I'm up to
Has a friend in Alfred whose name begins with an A	Has a friend in Aadam whose name begins with an A
He always thought about other people and not himself	I usually think about other people and not myself
Has LOTS of money	Needs LOTS of money

So what would Batman do?

Batman would:

- Stay close to the ground
- Keep his eyes open for enemies (Affa and Amma)
- Keep his ears peeled for every chance for his plan to work
- Have a plan first (mine needs working on)
- Be super stealthy so no one would suspect him
- Think quickly (because Affa is really good at that)
- Be like a ninja and stick to the plan (no changing my mind)

Now that I had all my skills prepared, I just needed to figure out how to stop Affa from marrying Umar Bhai and leaving us for good.

Operation 'Stop the Wedding' Ideas:

- Order a really expensive Xbox and lots of games with Affa's bank card so she doesn't have money for the wedding
- Sneak Umar Bhai a really ugly picture of Affa (I have PLENTY even one where she is picking her nose in nursery!)
- Make Umar Bhai hate our family so much that he has to say no to Affa
- Sneak Affa a really ugly picture of Umar Bhai (I could draw one)
- Tell Nanu that Umar Bhai is a dentist and will throw out her gwa fan

With a detailed plan and lots of ideas at the ready, all I had to do was take the first step. I took off Nanu's sandals to make it easier and dropped to the ground, just like Batman sometimes did. Amma always said that the best things always start off small and then grow into something bigger – just like me. So that's what I waited for: something small to get my mission up and running. Keeping my eyes open for enemies and my ears peeled for traps, I listened carefully for my next light-bulb moment.

I just didn't expect it to come so quickly...

CHAPTER THIRTEEN

"TAAAAAAAAAMMMMYYYYYY!"

Amma yelled from the bottom of the stairs. Her screams spiralled all the way up to my bedroom. "Can you make me and Nanu tea?"

"Coming!" Affa zipped passed me without even realising I was disguised on the landing like a lamp. STEALTH MODE had successfully been activated. Here I was: a martial arts master before I even turned ten years old. Just call me Batboy already.

True to my ninja-self, I crawled downstairs, trying to hide in the shadows of the wall. I knew every creak in the house so I could silently creep up on anybody and take them out if I had to. I was hoping it wouldn't come to that.

"Hello, Eesoof."

"AAAAAAAAAHHHHHHHHHHHH!"

I nearly jumped out of my skin and toppled down the stairs as Nanu prodded me with her walking stick. "Not again!" I squeaked. "Where on planet Earth did you come from?"

"Well, that depends," Nanu replied, using her walking stick to whack me away. "On my passport, it says—"

"Never mind," I said, rushing to my feet to inspect my limbs for battle wounds. For a teeny, tiny lady, Nanu sure was strong.

"Well," she said, manoeuvring me out of the way with her walking stick. "I better go speak to your sister about her training then. Today it's the 'Chaii Challenge.'"

"The what challenge?" I asked, dodging her swinging walking stick. She doesn't even need it, I swear. She just likes to hit people.

"Chaii, my dear boy." OH, she means Affa has to learn how to make the perfect cup of tea Not the English way with a kettle and a teabag either... life really isn't that easy.

Nanu's eyebrows joined forces and her forehead wrinkled. "By the time I could walk, I was an expert chaiiwala People used to come from all across the village for my sweet treats."

A chaiiwala is a tea-maker (and also

51

a really cool, grown-up, fancy pants cafe in town. I recommend the Desi breakfast)

Nanu must have learned how to walk really late because there was no way anyone would give boiling water to a baby – not even in Bangladesh.

"What's that got to do with Affa?"

"Well, to be a PERFECT wife, one must know the art of making THE PERFECT masala chaii. It has to be creamy and dreamy and steamy, with a dash of cinnamon, a pop of fennel seed, a pinch of love and–"

"I don't think you can buy love anywhere, Nanu," I interrupted. I was 99.93% sure that Umar Bhai didn't even drink tea, even if we DID have all the ingredients.

Nanu glared at me, scrunching up her red, crusty lips. "Chup! Don't speak such nonsense!" With that, she pottered downstairs, talking her walking stick with her.

"Chaii, my Eesoof," she called back, "is everything! It can make or break a marriage."

LIGHT BULB MOMENT #1

And there it was: my mission, should I choose to accept it (which I obviously did), was to sabotage the Chaii Challenge.

CHAPTER FOURTEEN

By the time I got to the kitchen, Affa had already put the milk on the stove. Even though there were only four people drinking it, she had used five teabags, which were all bleeding away and minding their own business. The secret, I'd learned long ago, was to use no water and an extra teabag.

"Budge up, kiddo." Affa said, popping in the fennel seeds. "You'll burn yourself."

I took a step back, a few actually, and sat on the kitchen table just between Affa's scarf and the Bombay mix. She already had a head start and the chaii was slowly frothing away, looking creamy and dreamy and steamy – just as Nanu said.

I took in a BIG whiff and my tummy rumbled. Oh man, this was the drink of Jannah. It just had to be, which meant that I had a lot of scheming to do. But the question was: when?

"TAAAAAAAAAMMMMMMMMMY,"

Nanu yelled from the living room. "I can't find the

Bangla news. It's gone!"

"COMING!" Affa called back. "Stay away from the pan, Yusuf. Okay?" Before waiting for an answer, she grabbed her scarf and dashed off.

This was my chance. I needed something truly disgusting to make sure that Affa failed Nanu's challenge.

I raided the drawers and found nothing. But deep in the cupboards, there was a rainbow of spices, nuts and leaves, pods and seeds, and lentils and chillies.

And there it was, smack bang in the middle of the rainbow: the ELASIES.

The black bits inside taste like smelly feet! YUCK!

PERRRRRRRFECT.

One of the worst things you can do in life is eat a mouth-watering chicken curry with all the potato, pepper and tomato trimmings only to find out you've bitten into one of these ABSOLUTE NASTIES. Once you've done that, that's it. There's no enjoying that curry ever again - no matter how long you spent sniffing it while Affa cooked. It could be worse though. MUCH WORSE.

One time, me, Affa and Amma were making samosas for Eid, and they decided to put me in charge of counting the elasies. What were they thinking? I ended up counting wrong and accidentally left an elasi in the chicken samosa mix – this was the fancy-pants mix too, the type we made for important guests only. We made 347 samosas that day and we've eaten 40 since. That means there's 1/307 chance that someone will bite into it. I say 'WILL' because it's still out there somewhere. WAITING. I can't wait to find out who gets it!

Focus, Yusuf. Focus. I flipped open the lid and plopped two, three, five – nope, TEN elasies into the mix. That should do it. Next I unscrewed the little box that Amma used to keep her precious things and looked for her most prized possession: a wild African ghost chilli. **MUHUHAHAHAHAHA!**

Usually, Amma kept one or two in her secret stash. It was the spiciest thing known to man. Affa once said that people actually died because it was too hot to handle and that's why they were called ghost chillies: men turned into ghosts after eating them, which is both creepy and cool, right? Amma and Nanu are always nibbling at them like mice, chewing a tiny bit at a time. But legend has it that Nana used to eat them whole just like they were

56

cheese and onion crisps. I wished so badly that I had been alive to see that.

But this time we were out, meaning that I needed another idea. I unscrewed a thousand more lids, sniffing for the answer, but everything just smelled so delightful! But wait! What was that?

It just so happened that right at the very back of the cupboard, between the deep-fried chicken feet and spicy peas, was an old, dusty tin. I peeled off the opening and found what had been waiting for me all along.

Inside lurked a sticky, brown menace. The smell wasn't as gross as I'd have liked, but if I was being honest, it looked like the inside of a nappy if the baby did an explosion of both a number one AND a number two. This, my friend, was excellent!

I quickly grabbed a spoon just as the sitting room door clicked shut. Oh no! Affa was coming. Only having time to drop one heaped sloppy spoon in, I slipped up and almost poured boiling hot chaii all over me.

AAAHHHHHHHH! Affa's footsteps got louder and louder and LOUDER. Code red! Code red! PANIC TIME!

And just as she slipped into the kitchen, I dove under the table, taking the tin of poop explosion with me, and disappeared out of sight.

CHAPTER FIFTEEN

Believe it or not, I had to crawl out of the kitchen when Affa turned around. While she was pouring the tea, without making a peep, I had to abandon the tin of poop and Batboy-mode all the way into the living room where I finally breathed like a human being again.

It was a VERY close call.

Amma had left a bowl of Bombay mix on the table here too, which meant that I could sit back, relax and make myself ready for the show.

While Affa clinked away in the kitchen, the news was on. Amma and Nanu listened carefully but I couldn't pay attention. Any second now…

Just then the door swung open and Affa came in. It was showtime. It's at times like this that I really wish there was a remote control for real life. That way I could play things in slow motion just like in Nanu's favourite Indian drama shows.

I quickly stuffed a handful of Bombay mix into my mouth and let the flavours explode on my tongue while Affa settled the tray down on the table. The chaii still smelled creamy and dreamy.

"Nanu?" I asked, passing the Bombay mix to her.

"No, no, my dear," she said, swatting me away. "I have more important matters to attend to. That mix will only meddle with my tastebuds." Nanu also didn't have ANY TEETH, which might have had something to do with it. My bad...

Affa placed a tea in front of Nanu, then Amma and then me before finally sitting back with one for herself. She blew into the cup to cool it down.

"Amma?" I asked, not once taking my eyes off Affa's lips.

She shook her hands and her bangles jingled. "You eat it, beta."

"Now," Nanu said slowly, picking up her cup. "Let's try this chaii, shall we?"

"If you must," Affa said, blowing harder at her own. She did it so hard that I'm pretty sure she nearly spat in it. Poor tea.

"The colour is just right," Nanu examined, scrunching up her enormous eyes just to make sure. "Not too dark and not too light." She swirled her cup and her glasses began to steam up. "The smell is very strong, just the way I like it." She took in a HUGE sniff – I was surprised the tea didn't SHOOT up her nose.

I shuddered at the thought while Affa pretended not to care and looked at the television.

"We need to cut down the guest list, Amma." Affa said, fiddling with the remote. "We can't afford to invite every Dawud, Mahmood and Ali."

Taking another handful of the mix, I chewed slowly so I didn't miss any important details over the sound of my loud **CRUNCH CRUNCH.**

"Don't worry, beti." Amma said, raising her own cup to her lips. "Your cousin Bilal's stepmum's aunty's friend's friend can't make it anymore so that's seven less. And remember that we're not inviting your mammi either so that's eight."

Mammis are aunties that get married to mamas (and mamas are brothers or cousin-brothers of your mum). It's very confusing, I know. I try not to think about it too much and just pretend I know what I'm talking about. I find nodding confidently helps. You should try it. I'm a pro now!

Affa groaned, but peered up quickly when Nanu cleared her throat.

The moment of truth: Nanu brought the cup to her lips and blew. For a split second, the steam cleared and ripples rolled through the tea. She blew again, and again, and again, smacking her lips like a chewing camel each time.

Come on, come on, Nanu! Come on!

Finally, she dipped her lips into the chaii and took a LOOOOONG, SLOOOOW **SLUUUUUURRRRRRRRRRRRRP**. Then she froze. She froze solid still. Even Affa and Amma turned around and stared at her.

"Farhana Begum," Nanu started, clearing her throat. Her voice was so high pitched that I thought maybe the cup in her hand would shatter. "WHAT IS THIS!?"

CHAPTER SIXTEEN

I tried not to smile, but it was SOOOOOOOOOOO hard that I had to jam-pack my WHOLE mouth with Bombay mix. **Yusuf 1: Affa 0.**

"Er, is everything okay, Nanu?" Affa put her tea down without taking a sip and muted the television. Her eyebrows began knitting themselves together.

The only sound came from Amma, who stopped slurping quickly, leaving only silence behind her.

Nanu muttered something, but I couldn't catch what.

SLLLUUUUUUUUURRRRRRRRPP. "This chaii, beti," she said in an almost whisper when she finished her sip, "has got to be THE BEST chaii I have ever tasted in my whole, entire life."

The Bomboy mix shot out of my mouth like November fireworks, spraying across the table. I tried not to choke as a little green seed soared out of my mouth and into Amma's tea.

"Yusuf!" They all shouted together as if they were triplets.

"I mean…" But wait, what did I mean? What the Jaffa cakes was going on? This didn't make any sense. I pulled my own cup closer and blew, taking a serious sip of chaii.

MA SHAA ALLAH.

This means 'what Allah wills' – I'm not really sure what that's got to do with anything, but Affa told me to say it when something is extra good. She says it too sometimes so it must be smart.

Oh, maaaaan! Nanu was right and I was a genius. I had just made the most perfect tea in existence and I didn't even know it. Affa, on the other hand, was beaming from ear to ear. So much for 'I'm too cool to care'.

I took another long sip. It was warm and smooth – and extra creamy and extra dreamy and extra steamy, with an explosion of love, a splash of cinnamon, a **POP!** of fennel seeds, and, and, and something I had never tasted before mingled in there too. Something sweet and light.

"Goo," Amma said, winking at her. "Nanu's secret ingredient."

WHAT? Did I hear right? "Goo?" The Bengali word for POO? Did I actually touch real-life poo? WAIT! Did we ALL just drink POO?

Desperate and in need of my inhaler – where was my inhaler? – I looked to Affa for help, but she was furrowing her eyebrows as if she was trying to remember doing something SHE DIDN'T ACTUALLY DO!

"Say it's not so, Affa. SAY IT'S NOT SO!" I cried. "Did we just drink GOO?"

Amma burst out laughing, spitting goo juice in my direction.

"IT BURNS US!" I hissed, quickly using my hands as a shield to protect myself. "IT BURNS US!"

"Calm down, Smeagol," Affa said, sipping her tea calmly, "Goor, not goo," she said.

"Goor?" I asked. What on planet Earth was that?

Amma took another sip. I hoped she didn't notice the little seed that fell in before. "Date molasses."

"Date who now?" Nanu piped in. "Who is dating in this house?" She was zooming in on Affa now and her walking stick was at the ready.

"No one is dating in this house, Nanu." Affa turned back to me. "It's brown."

"Who's brown?" Amma asked.

"Your son-in-law," Affa said to Amma, trying to ignore Nanu's glares. "And it's sticky."

"But I'M sticky!"

"Why are you sticky?" Amma snapped. "What have you done, Yusuf Ali Khan?"

"Does it look like a dried-up number one and number two explosion?" I asked seriously.

"Ewwwwww." Affa wriggled her nose. "That's disgusting, Yusuf.' She unmuted the news and listened to the presenter man nattering away. Affa was still smiling while Nanu sat back again and continued to drink. This must be the first time since she was born that Nanu has ever been nice to her.

"You should learn from your sister, Eesoof." Nanu grabbed her walking stick again and I bunched up closer to Amma for protection. "This young chaiiwala has a great future ahead. Haven't you, Tammy?"

"But, but," I started. "But wait—"

"No buts, Eesoof. Hush now. I'm trying to enjoy your sister's tea."

Affa's eyes lit up, but because she was still trying to play it cool, she didn't say anything back. All my clever tricks had gone down the pan – the chaii pan to be exact and Affa was sitting there smugly like my delicious masterpiece was her own. My heart sank: Yusuf 0 – Affa 1. At least I had the chaii of Jannah to make me feel better.

"TAMMMMMMMMY!" Nanu barked suddenly, making me spill my tea all over my trousers. Hot! HOT. HOT!

"Brides DO NOT smile!" Nanu shouted., shaking her walking stick at her. "Have you absolutely NO SHAME? Humble yourself, young chaiiwalla, otherwise people will think you're happy to leave us!"

Affa scowled and passed me a tissue from her pocket, trying to dab my legs dry.

"Here, have mine," she said, sliding her chaii to my side.

CORRECTION: Yusuf 0, Affa 1, Nanu 1.

CHAPTER SEVENTEEN

One of the things I love most about weddings (except from the food obviously) are the presents. Even though they're not mine, I like to see the shiny packages all wrapped up and pretend that some of them are actually for me.

For the ones I really want, I stare at them for a very long time and say nice things about them like 'I think those chocolates will tingle my tastebuds amazingly' or 'This waffle-maker should probably be plugged into our kitchen to test right now' or even 'That £300 will be very useful in the right hand' and I'll wave my right hand just to drop a hint. It doesn't always work, but I promise you, sometimes I've had some of those presents just thrown at me because of it. You should try it.

Today I'm helping Amma, Nanu and Affa wrap presents for Umar Bhai. His family are coming over later to drop off Affa's wedding dress. If you ask me, it's about time. She went to buy it with them ages ago.

If you're wondering why I'm helping by the way, it's because to be an excellent spy, you have to infiltrate enemy ranks and be a double agent. This Batboy won't get anywhere by giving up on the first try. No way. I have to be on the lookout for a back-up plan. And since half the sitting room was filled with baskets of sweets, treats and smellies, I was hoping one would just POP! into my head. But it really wasn't that easy.

"Yusuf?" Amma said, holding her fingers out. I was already ready with strips of tape for the sides of the basket.

When I say WE were wrapping all this, I really mean that I was the sellotape man. My job was a very important one: without me, everything would fall apart-literally. When somebody says 'Yusuf', I get my fingers down to business. I have to pull the exact amount of sellotape and give it carefully to the person who needs it. If the tape is too long, the work gets doubled and I have to chop it again and throw the extra bit away. If it's too short, then I have to start again entirely. It's not an easy job, but someone's got to do it.

"Yusuf," Affa said, measuring a red ribbon to the floor and curling it. It almost looked like her hair. I wondered if we could chop some of the red bits from Affa's head and use it if we ran out. "Can you just check that the smallest hamper by the fire has the watch box in it?"

I took the sellotape with me and covered my fingers with the sticky side so I didn't lose my spot.

Underneath the plastic, the watch glittered. Its hands ticked away silently on the small silver letters that read HUGE BOSS. Umar Bhai definitely was HUGE, but there's no way on planet Earth that he'd be able to boss Affa about. I'd pay good Jaffa cakes just to see him try.

"It's open," I said, staring at its face. "That watch would look absolutely excellent on the right hand, Affa." I waved my right hand (hint, hint).

"Nice try," she said, laughing.

It was worth a shot. I read the letters again. "When you get married, Affa," I asked, "are you not going to be the boss anymore? I find it really hard to believe that Affa would give up her bossy ways. Only God can help Umar Bhai. I don't think he thought this wedding thing through. Poor guy.

Amma chuckled and Nanu frowned, dropping her scissors on the spot.

"Of course she won't!" Nanu snapped, pulling her scarf over her head again. It had fallen off for the millionth time. It's a good thing she didn't see Affa roll her eyes. "The perfect wife knows never to speak unless she's spoken to! I don't know who these modern Londoni girls think they are, speaking to their husbands before their wedding day!"

By 'Londoni', Nanu means English.

"Nanu!" Affa dropped the ribbon and raised her voice. BAD move. BAD MOVE. Retreat, Affa. RETREAT! But she didn't, even though Amma quickly put a finger

72

to her lips and told her to SHUSH! She really does have no sense sometimes. "You're seriously telling me that you never spoke to Nana before you got married? SERIOUSLY?"

"Of course I did, silly girl," Nanu replied, pushing another basket towards her.

Affa's shoulders relaxed a little. Phew. Danger averted.

"We spoke on our wedding day," Nanu finished proudly.

Affa's eyebrows began to twitch. A time bomb was ticking.

CHAPTER EIGHTEEN

TICK TICK TICK went Affa's eyebrows. Her mouth began to twitch too. They were all like itchy caterpillars that were wiggling their bottoms.

Look here, I might not always be the best brother in the world, but I can definitely smell when trouble is brewing. My spidey senses were tingling and Affa, for once, needed saving. It was time to get her out of this sticky situation.

I scanned the room for a distraction. Television: no. Telephone: not this time. Cup of tea: not enough time. Chocolates: bingo!

"Wow wee, Nanu." Her attention was mine. Best brother medal, here I come. "Those fancy treats do look amazeballs. They would taste so elegant in my mouth right now." I didn't know what 'elegant' meant, but it sounded so good that Nanu actually turned her head.

"Eesoof, my dear," Nanu smiled toothlessly. It was kind of scary. "Nanu here is trying to give your sister some important wife lessons. Now be quiet!" She

74

snapped and rounded on Affa again. Amma, like a silent assassin, backed into the kitchen to put the kettle on, leaving me to watch the battle between the poisonous cobra and lizard-dragonoid continue.

"And why, my dear girl," Nanu didn't mean 'dear' in a nice way this time, "why in the world is your hair devil-red? Which shaytaan told you that was a good idea? Fear God and cover that with your— WAIT!" Nanu froze and scrunched her beady eyes.

UH OH! Affa noticed too and backed off. Sneakily, I took Nanu's scissors from the table (health and safety first – mainly Affa's health and safety). I was left with no other choice but to collapse onto the floor and pretend I was dead. It would be the only way.

This would hurt.

Ready?	No.
Steady?	Definitely not.
Go.	**BOOOOOM!**

"What the—" Affa started, hurrying towards me.

"EESOOOOOOOOOOOOOOOOOOOF!"

Thankfully, my head hit the soft bit of the sofa.

"Is my darling grandson still breathing, Tammy?" Nanu squealed hysterically. "Tell me he's still breathing!" Nanu spat out her gwa, spraying me with itty bitty red gunk. SUPER GROSS! "Let me give him mouth-to-mouth! It's the only way!"

"NOOOOOOOOOOOOOOOOOOOOOO— I mean, OWWWWWWW." Oh, boy. Just play dead, Yusuf. Just play DEAD.

"Yusuf," Affa said, patting my forehead. "You okay?"

Phew. They were still buying it.

"I…" This was a genius idea! I coughed dramatically for extra effect, but had to stop when my lungs nearly came out. "I…" I clutched my chest tightly. Now to take it to the next level. "I think…"

"Tell us what you think, Eesoof!" Nanu cried. "Don't be afraid!"

SHOWTIME.

"I think I need," I began weakly. "I think I need some really elegant chocolate."

Affa froze. "What?"

"Get the boy some chocolates, Tammy!" Nanu screamed. "What are you waiting for?!" Nanu tore open a chocolate platter and threw the Ferrero Rochers at Affa like bullets. "Feed him quickly! The milk will be good for him."

"Nanu that box was really expensive!" Affa tried to save the rest of the platter, but Nanu was having none of it.

"Do you care more about money or your brother's health?" I think we all know the answer to that.

"THESE," Affa said through gritted teeth. "They're not healthy!"

"If that's the case, why are you giving them to your husband-to-be?" There really was no winning with Nanu.

Affa sighed and threw me chocolates. Whoooop, whooooop!

Nanu started again. "And don't think I've not noticed that you don't have a scarf on. It belongs on your head, not your neck."

Oh, man. She remembered. So much for the distraction. At least both Affa and Nanu were calmer and no time bombs would detonate now.

Affa still wasn't happy. "Where in the rules does it say I have to wear my scarf 24/7? Tell me. If that was the case, I would have been born with it!"

Who would have thought that Affa could actually speak some sense?

"Nonsense!" Nanu argued, unwrapping a chocolate and sniffing it suspiciously. "A bride MUST do it - in the house, outside the house, always. Back in my day, we used to wear it in front of the television for fear that the men on the screen would see us."

I sat up, picking at another chocolate. "The television?" Maybe I should cough otherwise it'll be obvious I was faking it. I cleared my throat hard. That would do. I didn't want to overdo it, did I?

"Indeed." Nanu held her chocolate up to the window light to inspect it a little more.

Affa took it and bit it in half, giving Nanu the bigger piece back. "That's ridiculous." She said between mouthfuls. "Televisions weren't even invented then."

Just as Nanu slipped the little ball into her mouth, camel-chewing her way through it, and Amma came in to announce the tea, another LIGHT BULB moment hit me.

HEEEEELLLLLLLLLLLOOOOOOOOO, PLAN B!

CHAPTER NINETEEN

"I need your help," I told Aadam, shutting my bedroom door tightly.

Both he and Khala (AKA his mum AKA my aunty) had arrived all dressed up. Amma and Khala had forced us to match by making us wear identical cream kurtas over our jeans. We almost looked the same age now. Khala even said that we looked like young Amitabh Bachchans in the making.

"What's the plan, Batman?" Aadam hopped onto the bed, pushing the hanging bandages away.

"We have a HUGE challenge on our hands," I explained, picking some fluff off a chocolate that I'd saved and passing it to him. "We have 25 minutes and 28 seconds to get rid of ALL the scarves in this building. Every single one of them."

Adam peeled off the gold wrapper and filled his whole mouth with chocolate. "I don't get it," he crunched. "How is that going to stop the wedding?"

"Well, Umar Bhai's brother and uncles are coming today and there's no way Affa will come downstairs without a scarf."

Aadam's eyes widened. "Ohhhh, I see. If she doesn't come, they'll think she's bald."

"No, they'll—"

"Think she's got eyes on the back of her head." Aadam interrupted.

"NOOOOOO—"

"That she has snakes for hair?"

"NO! Listen, they'll think she's rude and not wife material," I finished finally.

"That was my next guess." Sometimes, for a wise old egg, Aadam can be well, NOT so wise.

"Sure it was. Anyway, what say you, Robin?"

Aadam thought about it for a whole five seconds and then jumped to his feet. "Count me in!"

YES!

"Okay," I looked at my imaginary watch. "We have 23 minutes and 47 seconds to gather everything. There are about twenty trillion scarves in a million different colours in almost every corner of this house.

We'll have to put them under Nanu's bed. She's got the most space."

Aadam opened the door and peeked outside.

"She's in the shower." I said. "She was cleaning the toilet when I last saw her."

"Gross."

"I know," I nodded. Time was running out. "We need to be smart. How about I take Affa's room, and you take Amma and Nanu's."

Before Aadam could answer, we heard footsteps on the stairs. They were getting louder and louder and closer and closer. Affa skipped lightly so it couldn't be her. Nanu had three slow feet (including her walking stick) so it couldn't be her. And Amma's were heavier so it DEFINITELY wasn't her.

Aadam glared at me in horror, his arms were shaking. "Yusuf," he whispered. "She knows."

At that very second, Khala **BOOOOOOMED** through the door, sending it swinging wildly on its hinges. Wearing a black sari and a black scarf to match, she looked exactly like the grim reaper, coming to take us both.

"I know," she muttered darkly, jingling her gold bangles. It was a warning sign. It had to be.

We both became statues, trying not to give anything away.

Khala began again even slowly. "I know exactly what you two troublemakers need." She lifted the flap of her sari and brought out a huge bowl. I was sure there was a slipper in there somewhere.

"Chicken samosas!" she said brightly.

"CHICKEN SAMOSAS!" Me and Aadam squealed together, jumping up and down and swapping high fives.

"Thanks, Khala." I said, breathing normally now. PHEW! Close call.

"You're the best, Mum!"

"I know, beta," she said, pinching our cheeks and leaving the bowl with us as she swept out of the room. "Tell your dad that, will you, love?"

CHAPTER TWENTY

By the time we finished our samosas, we only had 14 minutes left to complete our mission. Thankfully, that was just enough time to raid every drawer and every corner of the house.

"We did it!" Aadam squealed, staring at the rainbow of scarves stashed under the bed.

Nanu's room was like a tiny dustbin. It had a small bed, a smaller wardrobe and an even smaller window, as well as almost a thousand years' worth of artefacts from her life. My favourite one was her box of kidney stones. She had them taken out ages ago and kept them safe in her chest of drawers. Anyway, It was a miracle we both fit into her room. It was even more of a miracle that we could breathe over the stinky smell of old mothballs.

"I wish we could swim in it," I said, imagining myself doing a butterfly stroke in the sea of multicoloured scarves. "Are you sure you got all of-"

DING DONG! DING DING DONG!

"They're ON TIME!" Aadam said, hopping on the bed and peeking through the blinds at the window. "Affa's new family actually know how clocks work!" He paused. "Woah, look at them all."

I ran to the window beside him, pushing away the other half of the blinds. Aadam was right. I had to rub my eyes twice, but he sure was right.

Outside our house was an Audi, a Mercedes, a BMW and a blue car. "Cooooooool."

"Dibs on the Audi," Aadam said, watching as people spilled out of its doors, carrying baskets and bags of mitai.

The most delicious sweet snacks in the universe. My favourites are the red gulab jamuns (hint, hint).

"Dibs on the blue one." If my eyes weren't lying, which I'm 95% sure they weren't, I counted nine people coming out of it. That was almost a whole football team in that little clown car.

"EESOOOOOOOOOOOOOOOF!

AAAAAADDAAAAAAAAAAAMMM!"

Nanu called. "Get your bottoms here FAST! We need to keep them busy. Your mother is still in the shower!"

"Coming." I yelled back. On our way, I was almost sure that I heard Affa whisper my name from upstairs. Adam stopped dead in his tracks. He had heard it too. I had to pull him forward as butterflies filled my tummy. "Come on," I said loudly, pretending not to hear her.

DING DONG. DING DING DONG.

Something told me it was too late to turn back now. Gulp. I'd have to see my plan though no matter what. At least if I got in big trouble, this time Aadam would be going down with me, which made me feel a little bit better. Maybe I could pin the whole thing on him? No, there's no way I could do that to him.

"Get the door, Eesoof." Nanu said, redoing her scarf by the mirror in the hallway. "Your khala's frying the pakoras and rolls. Why in God's name are they so early?"

"I think only God knows that," Aadam said helpfully. "Maybe you should ask Him."

Nanu almost threw her walking stick at us. "Maybe you should get the door!" she hissed.

So, as the smell of fried goodness wafted through the hall, I held my breath and opened the front door, praying my plan would work.

CHAPTER TWENTY-ONE

"As-salaamu'alaikum."

This means 'peace be upon you' and I say it like I say 'hello there!'

I had to say it to each and every person, so 24 times, and Nanu STILL asked me if I said it to everyone - even the sleeping babies. Everyone who could talk answered 'wa alaikum as-salaam' back- including the last one, who turned out to be a delivery driver, dropping off our neighbour Ms Hayley's parcel (she was away for the holidays).

All the guests rolled into the sitting room, piling their parcels and presents on me. Normally, this would have been a dream come true, but I was running out of hands and I could only balance so much on my head before—

CRAAAAASSSHHHHHHHH!

Oh well, at least it was only the soy feeta thaal. They didn't really taste of anything anyway. It could have been much worse, right? I kicked the snacks underneath the shoe-rack before anyone could even notice.

In the hallway, Umar Bhai's family were glittering with every colour under the sun. I bet I could find a scarf upstairs to match each one.

Yasin Bhaiyyah was the only boy I knew. He was Umar Bhai's brother and he was in high school. Bhaiyyah definitely looked a lot cooler in his kurta than we did. He must have had a haircut too because it looked VERY fresh.

"Did you just give salaam to that delivery guy? Just cause he's brown, bruv, it doesn't mean he's blood." He laughed as he clicked the door shut behind him, setting down the box beside the tiny mountain of shoes that had appeared in the last five minutes. "You get me?"

"I didn't see any blood." I would have noticed a bleeding man, wouldn't I? "But he was wearing a turban though."

"Safe," Yasin Bhaiyyah said, nodding seriously. "Safe, little man. You good. You good."

I pointed to the sitting room, hoping he would go in that direction. Cool people must speak a whole different language because I had no idea what he was saying.

"Why does he keep saying 'safe'?" I sneakily asked Aadam. Nothing dangerous was happening here (unless you counted Nanu).

Aadam thought for a second. "I think he means that we're safe now that the door's closed and we're outside of the danger zone. I think I heard a dog before. It must be coming our way."

"That makes sense," I nodded. Aadam was deathly afraid of dogs. Once I looked out of the front room window only to see an Aadam-shaped asteroid blasting past our house. It turned out Ms

Hayley's shih tzu, Peagreen, was sleeping in the garden.

Like a laser, I felt Nanu's eyes on me before I saw them.

"This is Eesoof," I heard Nanu say to two old women in huge cardigans. "Ma shaa Allah, he's such a good boy, always looking after his Nanu. Aren't you, my little Eesoof?"

Only she could say God's name and then tell a complete lie straight afterwards. Wasn't that bad? I smiled and nodded before quickly turning back around to Aadam. But somehow, I just KNEW that Nanu was still staring at me with her beady little eyes. I could still feel them on me.

Maybe Nanu wanted me to look at her. That had to be it. There were people around so this was still a safe zone for now. I turned around slowly to see her scrunch up her lips and grab a tight hold of her walking stick. Oh no. Had she just heard my thoughts? Had she? Could she read minds? Panic time! SHE HAD JUST HEARD MY THOUGHTS! NANU COULD HEAR THOUGHTS!

I hid behind Aadam who was laughing really loudly and trying to impress Yasin Bhaiyyah, but it was too late. Nanu was coming for me.

"Eesoof!" She tugged my ear, whispering furiously. "Where is your sister? She should be here by now!"

"Affa? Right now? Um, I don't know where she is…" That was the truth, the whole truth and nothing but the truth! Don't look at me like that! I mumbled into Nanu's ear as an extremely elegant thaal passed us. It was wrapped with sparkly foil and shimmered. What? At least, I wasn't lying about Affa-ooooh chocolate! "Erm Nanu, can I have my ear back?" There'd be no way to get to it with a nanu attached to me.

The two women in huge cardigans were staring at us and Nanu knew it. We were being watched.

"Oh look at my little, handsome beta," Nanu said loudly. "He's still giving his Nanu noonoos even though he's getting so tall."

Oh NO! Just like that, all my cool points disappeared. Aadam was shaking his head and Yasin Bhaiyyah was giggling through his braces.

But that was the least of my problems because Nanu had suddenly grabbed my cheeks and was pinching them! OUCH!

"You go get your sister before her wedding turns into a funeral!" Nanu hissed, still smiling at the other guests. "My Eesoof is so cute," she continued loudly. "Now go! Don't come back without her!"

CHAPTER TWENTY-TWO

Dead.

That was me.

At least that was GOING to be me in a few minutes when either Affa or Nanu got a hold of me. I didn't know who I was more scared of and I definitely didn't want to find out.

I was halfway up the stairs with absolutely no back-up plan. If I continued to go up and found myself in a face-off with Affa, she'd suss me out in a heartbeat.

If I went to Nanu empty-handed, with no Affa in sight, she'd probably throw chilli powder in my eyes and blind me.

If Amma found out, she'd explode. She would just EXPLODE. I'd have to pick up the pieces of her afterwards.

What could I do now? Where could I even hide? How did I want to spend the very last hours of my—

"EESOOOOF!"

My heart jumped into my throat and knocked me off my feet. I tumbled, tumbled, tumbled all the way down the stairs and smashed clean into the mountain of shoes by the front door.

RINGING.

My ears were ringing. I tried to lift my head up slowly, but it was so heavy that it flopped back into the river of shoes. I was drowning! I was being gassed by the suffocating stench! The weight and stink of the shoes almost dragged me under. Worse still, a high heel had stabbed me in the back and a smelly sock wriggled into my mouth. Goodbye, cruel world. This was the last of Yusuf Ali Khan.

When I woke up, I saw a blurry, grey bunny rabbit in front of me. Amma was yelling at the bunny and Nanu was shaking it. Then the bunny rabbit put my spectacles on my face and turned into Affa in that instant.

It turned out that I wasn't looking at a bunny rabbit at all. It was Affa. She was wearing a grey hat and scarf.

"Are you okay, Yusuf?" ~~The bunny~~ Affa asked.

I looked around. A million pairs of eyes were staring at me silently. Oh boy, this was not a good sign.

I nodded slowly, throwing away the pink high heel that had tried to take my life.

"Affa?" I asked.

"Yes, kiddo?" A trillion beads of sweat trickled down her face. She was that worried about me!

I knew she loved me!

"Why are you wrapped in a winter hat and scarf right in the middle of summer?" I knew she was weird too. I just didn't think Affa was this weird.

Affa stiffened, remembering where she was. Her cheeks started growing pink and Amma's face went from 'poor Yusuf' to 'you'll pay for that, Yusuf' in about ten seconds flat.

Nanu cleared her throat. "Nothing to see here. Absolutely nothing at all." She got up, using her walking stick to help her. "My little Eesoof just had a little fall, didn't you, beta? And my daughter's daughter," she said, looking at Affa like she had grown another head. When Nanu's extra mad at us, she likes to pretend she's not related to us as much. "She feels a little under the weather. Why else would anyone wrap up so ridiculously in the dry heat of summer?"

Then it hit me. The plan! YEEEEESSSSSSS!

Yusuf 1: Affa: 1

CHAPTER TWENTY-THREE

"Yusuf Ali Khan!" Amma hissed in my ear while pretending to help me up from the mountain of shoes. "You better fix this now, fwa, or else."

Amma gave me the stink-eye, pinching me under the arm (OUCH!). She turned around and smiled at everyone else. "Londoni boys these days," she said laughing. But that wasn't a real laugh. It was a DANGER ZONE laugh - one that was electric.

Uh oh. It was coming. The mighty Amma-zap was coming.

Thank God there were eyewitnesses. There was absolutely no way that Amma would attack in broad daylight in front of a whole bunch of people. No way would she do that. What would people say? No, I've known Amma my whole life. I was safe. For now.

Wasn't I?

"He'll be fine," Khala yelled from the kitchen. The clinking of plates and pans echoed into the hall. DID SHE EVEN KNOW WHAT HER SISTER WAS CAPABLE OF?!

Everyone's heads turned that way except Aadam's. He just stared at me from behind Yasin Bhaiyyah's arm and drew his finger deathly straight across his neck. Even worse, the remnants of a samosa clung to his collar. He had eaten a chicken delight without me.

"Dead man," Aadam mouthed, shaking his head. "You're a dead man."

Something told me he was right.

I turned to see Amma shooing Affa upstairs. The huge bunny hopped all the way out of sight just as Khala yelled, "Food's ready! Come on, everybody."

Bad timing. BAD TIMING! BAD TIMING!

There was a huge surge towards the kitchen. The old ladies and big kids made their way there in waves, leaving me out here with Amma alone (with an enormous pile of weapons of mass destruction: the shoes). For once, Amma had plenty to choose from. I bit my lip and smiled sheepishly. There was no way I'd survive this. No way at all.

"Yusuf!" Aadam whispered behind Amma's back.

Aadam's eyes grew wide and he froze. This had to be what Nanu called 'The Fear of God'.

"Promise me something," he said, looking over his shoulder to see if Amma was coming, but she was still distracted shooing everyone politely into the kitchen. We only had seconds for our final goodbye.

"Anything, Aadam. Anything." I wanted to tell him that he was the real-life brother I always wanted. I wanted to say that without him, I wouldn't have had a best friend. I wanted to tell him that it was me who ate the last gulab jamun in his fridge last summer. But the words were stuck in my throat.

Aadam held tight to my shoulder.

"Promise me," he said quietly. "Promise me you won't drop me in it," he cried. "And promise I can keep your tablet." He held me tighter.

"I promise, I promise, I— Wait, WHAT?"

But at that very moment, Amma turned back around.

"Well, it was nice knowing you," he added brightly before trailing after Yasin Bhaiyyah.

GULP.

Before I could make a break for it, Amma quickly pinched my ear, pinning me to the spot.

It was coming. IT WAS COMING! LEVEL FOUR OF ANGRY WAS COMING! I REPEAT LEVEL FOUR! MAN DOWN! MAN DOWN!

"You listen to me right now, Yusuf Ali Khan. Do I have 'idiot' written on my forehead?" Amma was hissing. For a second, instead of double-checking the gap between Amma's scarf and eyebrows, I made sure that she hadn't evolved into a giant man-eating python. It was hard to tell, especially when she started spitting in anger.

Amma waited for the kitchen door to close and then she pulled me closer. She was so close that I could feel her slow breath against my cheek.

Forget butterflies in my stomach – I had a swarm of bees and they were attacking me from the insides.

"Now you listen to me carefully, Yusuf." Amma growled. "If you want to see the next five seconds alive, you will do exactly as I say. You hear me, fwa?"

I nodded slowly. Our noses were almost touching, and I tried not to focus on the leftover onion bhaji stuck in her teeth. Amma's hand was still attached to my ear so making any sudden movements could be fatal.

"You march right up those stairs and undo whatever it is that you've done. Is that clear?"

Without waiting for me to answer, Amma grabbed my arm and dragged me up the stairs. We were moving further and further away from the safety of civilisation and moving closer and closer to the mouth of terror. And I wasn't talking about Amma's onion breath.

"Help me." I squeaked. "Somebody help me!"

CHAPTER TWENTY-FOUR

Amma glared at me and folded her arms. Was it just me or did she look exactly like a hypnotised racoon with eyes locked on its prey? We were in Nanu's room and Affa (who had lost her ears and fluffy tail) shut the door silently and sealed us all in. The two of them were true criminals indeed, trying to leave no trace of the crime scene while a whole party went on downstairs. If the swarm of bees from before hadn't stung my heart and left it for dead, this would have been soooooooooooo cool.

"Give them to me," Affa snarled, grabbing Nanu's table lamp and pointing it at me like a spear. Her hair must have started melting in the hat because it stuck to her head like fresh slime.

I backed into Nanu's bed, feeling for the blanket just in case I needed it as a weapon. If the worst happened, I could just trap them, run and think about the rest later.

"Yusuf, do as she says," Amma said, looking at the lamp like it might explode. She moved between us, putting her life on the line to become a human shield. Maybe she did love me after all. SHOW ME THAT LOVE, AMMA. SHOW IT TO ME!

But wait, was she protecting me or was she protecting Affa? I couldn't trust any of them.

Just then Affa **ZAPPED** in front of me, destroying my safety bubble. I was TRAPPED between her and the bed. Even the BED was on her side!?

"What you going to do with that?" I asked. This was no time to break eye contact, BUT I REALLY NEEDED TO BLINK.

"I'm going to shove it—"

"Ey, furi," Amma warned.

Just like 'fwa', 'furi' means girl —
not in the nice way either.

"But AMMMMMMMMMMA." Affa began, swinging the light bulb dangerously close to my face.

"Chup, beti!" Amma raised her hand like a knife, making Affa take a step back. "The best of us are those who are best in character, and the best of them are those who are best to their—"

"Amma! My future in-laws are downstairs! We don't have time for this!"

"Farhana Begum!" Amma said sternly. "Let me handle this."

HOLY SNOWBALLS! Let Amma handle this? NO WAY! YAA RABB, SAVE ME FROM THIS DARKNESS AND BRING ME INTO LIGHT!

I didn't know what that meant, but Amma used to say it all the time when she was ill. Somehow it made everything better. Maybe it'd help now, too.

"ARRRRGHHHHH!" Affa stomped her feet and pulled the lamp so hard that it actually switched on.

Dear Lord, that wasn't what I meant.

"Yusuf Ali Khan," snapped Amma.

I felt dizzy. I was going to be sick right there and then. My hands shook and I had to cross my legs tightly just in case anything leaked. Be calm. Be calm. BE CALM BE CALM BE CALM. I got this. I could explain that it was a mistake. I could say I did it because I loved Affa so much that I didn't want her to go. I could just tell them that this was all a mistake.

"IT WAS NANU! SHE MADE ME DO IT!"

Who said that? WHO said that? WHO ON THE WHOLE OF PLANET EARTH, THE GALAXIES AND BEYOND SAID THAT? I looked around and Affa and Amma just stared at me blankly.

"Yusuf, how could you say that?" Affa said, slamming the lamp on the table. "How could you lie like that?"

OH, MAAAAAAAAAAAAAAAN.

"You better start getting out those scarves in the next three seconds," Amma interrupted. They were tag-teaming now, ignoring the fact that my hands were up and I had surrendered already. There was no escape. None whatsoever.

"Three…" Amma started.

"You are this close to getting a black eye," Affa added.

"Two…"

Without taking another breath, I stopped, dropped and rolled out the evidence from under Nanu's bed.

CHAPTER TWENTY-FIVE

"Wa alaikum asalaam," Nanu and Amma said for the fifteenth time as they waved goodbye to everybody in the hallway. They hugged all the grown-ups and old people again, but still they all stood rooted to the spot. Nobody was moving towards the door just yet.

Yasin Bhaiyyah, Aadam and three of the other bhais actually sat on the bottom steps, watching their seventh Ali Official video. I gave it twelve and a half more minutes before anybody actually opened the front door

"Bruv, bruv, bruv, naaaah," Yasin Bhaiyyah yelled as the others howled with laughter. "They're always like 'Not even water?!' Duh!"

"Nah, fam," the other bhai called, waving his hands. He had Amma's squiggly signature shaved into the side of his head. I desperately wanted to draw on it. "My favourite one's "You don't eat for a WHOLE month!'"

"It's so jokes man, innit?" Aadam said. "Bare safe, bruv."

Oh maaaaan, even Aadam spoke a different language now. It was too late. He'd gotten cooler without me.

Affa and Khala were standing by the kitchen, playing it cool and giggling with another aunty while I was stuck behind the railings of the stairs.

"Act normal," Amma had told me when we all finally marched down the steps like my life hadn't just been threatened.

Act normal? How was I supposed to act normal when I didn't even know if I'd survive the next few hours? I couldn't even remember what normal felt like, so I just sat on the stairs and prayed I'd melt into the carpet so everyone would forget I was in trouble.

"Aadam!" I whispered, trying to get his attention. Maybe he could solve this. He knew what normal looked like, right?

"AHAHAHAHAHAHAHAHAHA,"

Aadam bellowed, slapping his face like a chimpanzee. "Yes! Safe, bruv."

Okay, maybe not.

"In shaa Allah everything goes well next week," one of the old fossils in a cardigan said while chewing away on gwa faan. "I'm so blessed to have a new granddaughter-in-law who cares so much about her family – especially that little one." The new nanu pointed at me. "What will he do without her?"

Say what now? WHAT WILL I DO WITHOUT HER? You mean what will SHE do without ME? Affa didn't care about anybody – especially us! How come she was always the hero of the story? We'll see about that.

"AND she almost smashed a lamp on my head!"

Nanu's eyes snapped in my direction. Wait, wait! Which bit just escaped from my mouth?

"And she always dashes out for bread because Yusuf loves bread." Amma said quickly.

Phew! Good save, Amma. (Now I just needed somebody to save me!)

Nanu nodded. "Such a lovely God-fearing girl. Tammy makes the nicest chaii, you know. She can run a household, cook and clean, and make THE PERFECT handesh – all round and sweet and fluffy. God has really blessed her, ma shaa Allah."

Handeshes are the yummiest sweet treats – the best way to eat them is by dunking them in warm milk and runny cream. We only ever make them on special occasions.

I looked at Affa in shock, who looked at Nanu, who was now looking at me.

At that exact moment, somebody opened the door and let the night inside.

"Oh, it's getting dark," Khala said in her 'IT'S-TIME-TO-GO' voice. "We better get going. Aadam, get your shoes on."

"But Muuummmm," Aadam started, peeling his eyes away from the mobile phone.

"We should go too," the other-other new nanu said.

And with that, the whole house emptied like a 30 second sand-timer, leaving me, Affa and Amma all on our own.

Dear God,

Please keep me alive.

CHAPTER TWENTY-SIX

Amma gave me three punishments:

No tablet or T.V. until I deserved it (I hugged it goodbye before Amma dragged it off me, telling me that I had to learn how to let things go. It would be a whole, long while before I saw that again.)

I'd have to handwash all of Affa's scarves because they stunk of mothballs after spending a whole two hours in Nanu's room (and because there was an old, half-eaten samosa wrapped tightly inside one of them, a bottle of drippy chocolate sauce in another and my smelly P.E. sock in one more. How did they even get there?) Don't worry. I ate it. Nanu raised me to never waste food.

I sat in my room, staring at the bandages on my arm. If you're wondering, no, Affa didn't break my bones, and she didn't help me put my bandages on either. This was the SECOND time she did that and today was the day I needed her the most.

After everyone had left, punishment number three started – I didn't forget that one, see!

Amma made me:

- brush the floor
- wet-tissue-wipe the tables
- take the bin outside (SUPER GROSS)
- turn the cushions so they were the right way round
- tidy the shoes
- lock the door
- pick the stamped on feeta from the floor
- complain a bit (okay, I did this because I wanted too)
- put all the dry dishes away ONE MEASLY PLATE AT A TIME (only Nanu ever did it like that and she only did her own)

And do you know how long everything took? Millenniums! It took millenniums! So now all I could do was sit on my bed, too tired to even swing my legs. My back was all achy, my fingers were claws and even my toes had given up. They just looked towards the ceiling really sadly like they had been in trouble too.

And Affa had forgotten Zombie Yusuf. There'd be no dead bodies, no mad scientists and no burials. Not even mine.

After everything had been done and I had crawled out of the kitchen, Affa just went upstairs without even a thank you. Not one word. Nothing. Zilch. Total silence. That's right. You heard right! A 'good, granddaughter-in-law', my butt. What would people say?

I froze. That sounded familiar…

Uh oh.

It was finally happening! ! I was turning into Nanu! **NOOOOOOOOOOOOOOOO.**

I ran to the mirror, tripping up on a loose bandage roll on the way. Barely keeping my balance, I turned to face the monster in the glass. His eyes were pink, his back was hunched, and his eyebrows were angry.

"No," I repeated over and over again, pulling my face to hide the wrinkles. "This can't be happening. I'm hideous. Hideous, I tell you!"

I looked more closely in the mirror. Did I look smaller? WAS I SHRINKING?

I ran out of my room and nearly crashed straight into Affa's door. Luckily, I stopped myself right in the nick of time. Just as I was about to storm in, I heard voices on the other side. They were laughing and talking and being a family without me.

Pressing my ear hard above the handle, I listened carefully.

"—can't believe I finally get to wear it," Affa squealed.

I closed my eyes and imagined I was in there. Affa must have been wearing her dress, twirling round and round like a washing machine.

"I can't believe it's taken so long to make," Nanu said. "Eight whole weeks! In my day, you could pay for it and wear it on the same day."

"Mine too, remember, Ma? I think I still have mine in the attic somewhere." Amma must have sat down because the bed had started to creak. "You look beautiful, beti, so very beautiful."

"Just like I did," Nanu said. "Don't you go looking too beautiful, my dear, lest you leave with four husbands instead of one!"

Affa and Amma laughed.

"What will I do without you, Nanu?"

"No, beti." Nanu said quietly. "What will we do without you?"

CHAPTER TWENTY-SEVEN

"You owe me big time," I told Aadam the next day.

We were in the garden because Khala said we all needed some vitamin D before next week. The sun was so bright that we could actually starfish backwards onto the grass and look like spies in our shades and weapons. Aadam didn't know it, but it was all part of my big plan to get revenge.

Soon it was quiet. Perfectly quiet. I waited for just the right moment for the birds to stop speaking, for the grass to sit still and for the smell of Amma's naan to waft up our nostrils and tickle our nose hairs.

Naan is a big round flat bread, but it's light and fluffy and the best flavours are spicy keema (mince) and sweet garlic.

Then it was game on.

I took a deep breath and prepared to deactivate stealth mode.

It was almost time.

I was ready.

Three…

Two…

One!

"YOU BETRAYED THE CODE, SOLDIER!"
I screamed, pouncing to my feet.

Aadam squealed and grabbed his pistol. His
sunglasses slipped down from his chest onto the grass.

"YOU LEFT ME FOR DEAD!" I shouted, aiming the water-gun at him. "YOU SIDED WITH THE ENEMY, YOU ENEMY-SIDER! You even know their language," I spat. "Do you feel 'safe' now? Huh? Huh?"

Aadam was shaking. There was a dark patch in the middle of his shorts. Had he... oh, his water-gun was leaking. FOCUS, YUSUF, FOCUS!

"It's not what you think," he said, holding tightly to his pistol. He raised a hand to surrender, but didn't let go of his weapon. "Wait, Yusuf. I can explain."

"Go on, then. Explain." I said, looking him directly in the eye. "Explain how you betrayed your best friend and hid behind enemy lines. Explain how you sold out your own bhai. Tell me, I tell you! Tell me!"

He started to get up. "I was just-"

"STAY DOWN!" I shouted, holding tightly to the trigger. "Don't make me do something I don't want to do."

"Yusuf, listen," he said desperately.

"I am listening!"

"I don't know what to say," Aadam lowered his gun and dropped it on the grass.

"How can I ever trust you again?" I yelled. "You were supposed to be my friend!" My voice rang through the garden. Aadam Mahmoud was on my turf now.

"Yusuf, Yusuf! Look at me!"

This was a trap. It had to be.

Aadam's hands were digging into his pockets. Did he have another weapon? Would he take me down with him?

"Hands where I can see them. Now now now!" I pushed the gun towards him, but he didn't back down. "Bad move, Aadam. Bad move. Do as I say. Now!"

But he didn't. Instead he just smiled. Aadam was a double agent! He had to be!

"Say hello to my little friend," he said, pulling a suspicious package out of his pockets.

CHAPTER TWENTY-EIGHT

"INCOMING! INCOMING!" I screamed, turning around as Aadam targeted the package in my direction. Holding tightly to the gun, I stormed towards the other side of the garden, aiming to dive behind Amma's khodu pots.

"JAFFAAAAAAAAAAAAAAAAAAAA BOMB!" Aadam yelled as the **WHOOOOOOOSH** of a grenade sliced through the air.

"AAAAAAAAAAAHHHHHHHHHH!"

Wait! A JAFFA what? Could it be? No... but could it?

I spun on the spot, aiming my pistol at the bomb. A huge orange space-shell was soaring towards me. I quickly raised my gun and pressed down on the trigger.

SWOOOOOOOOOOOOSH! A jet of water exploded from my –

CRAAAAAAASSSSSHHHHHHH!

Tumbling, stumbling and rumbling, I went through pots and plants, and stems and nets, and bamboo sticks then SMACK! The orange space-shell plopped straight onto my head, knocking my glasses off and making me all woozy.

But the khudo vines were ALIVE! They were alive, I tell you. ALIVE! The green claws snatched my arms, taking me under like quicksand. I tried to break free, but it was too strong. Huge leaves crawled over my face, trying to suffocate me! Amma's baby khudos were dying to suffocate me! Suddenly, they didn't look so innocent after all!

"My baby!" screamed Amma. Her voice was like an angel echoing from Jannah. It rang through the air and made me feel warm and fuzzy.

But not for long. I tried to keep my head up, tried to gasp for air. If Amma didn't get to me soon, I'd be a goner.

"Yusuf, noooooooo!" the traitor called. "Save yourself! Don't go under. I repeat, DO NOT GO UNDER."

But it was too hard. The vines had already strapped themselves around my legs, coiling like snakes, refusing to let go. The leaves stuck to my face, forcing its way up my nose. I tried to blow it away, but I was getting weaker and weaker by the second.

"My baba. Is my baba okay?"

Finally, Amma loosened the green goblins and I could breathe again. She swept the leaves away from my face and I could see again.

"I'm okay," I said, breathing hard. "I'm okay."

"Are you okay, baba?" Her voice rang through the wooziness. "Such a nasty fall you had."

I searched for my glasses and returned them to my face. "Alhamdullilah, I'm fine, Amma. I'm fine," I said, dragging myself up.

Nanu makes me say this every time I survive a near-death experience, which is a LOT with her around. It's to show that I'm grateful for, you know, still breathing and other things.

But then I saw BLOOD on my knee! The pot had attacked me! IT HAD ATTACKED ME!

"Amma, look! The pot!"

"SSHH, Yusuf!" She snapped as Aadam ran over to us.

"You okay, Yusuf?" he breathed, crouching down.

"Yeah, yeah." I inspected my knee. I was okay, I think.

"Erm, Khala," Aadam had turned to Amma, who must have been behind me. "Are you okay?"

I swung around to see Amma cradling her baby khudos, shushing the little green bottle plants to sleep. "You're okay, baba," she whispered to them. "You're okay."

She had been talking to THEM the ENTIRE TIME.

CHAPTER TWENTY-NINE

"Sometimes I think our mums are the same person, I swear," Aadam said, peeling apart a half-moon Jaffa cake.

We'd dissected the orange grenade on the sitting-room table and discovered that the insides had exploded. It must have happened when it smashed into my head. See, I knew I was as hard as snails.

"She's done it before," I said, chomping on the chocolate shrapnel. It still tasted GOOOOOOOOOOOOOOD. "There was one time when I fell down the stairs and bust my toenail. Amma saved her naga plant and left me to die."

"Mum does it, too." Aadam said. He shuffled on the sofa, wiggling his butt so he could get comfy. "I got you something else as well."

"YOOOOOOOOOOOOOOOOOOOU DID?" I squeaked, jumping up and clapping. Aadam is the KING of gadgets. His dad buys him EVERYTHING. All he has to do is just look at it and it's his. The Jaffas splattered across the table. Play it cool, Yusuf. Play. It. Cool. "I mean, safe." I nodded seriously. Much better.

"Yep, look." He hopped off the sofa (all that wiggling went to waste) and reached for his bag in the corner of the room.

Be. cool. BE COOL.

I tried to pretend not to be interested. He did betray me after all. It would take a lot more than some measly Jaffa cakes and whatever else to be my sidekick again. Especially after yesterday.

Aadam turned back around.

"AAARRRRGHHHHHH!"

We both yelled at the exact same time. I tried my best not to have an asthma attack.

For some reason, Aadam's nose was less than a millimetre away from mine. My legs obviously didn't listen to my brain when I ordered them to stay put. Instead the little traitors followed him to the corner.

"I didn't hear you get up!" Aadam gasped, his eyes going back to human size.

"Neither did I!" Where was my inhaler? Why did I never have it on me?

"Look, Yusuf. I know I did a dirty and sold you out," he started again, uncrushing the carrier bag in his hands. "But I won't do it ever again."

Of course he was never going to betray me again, because I was never going to let him be my number one best friend again. He'd just have to be my second best friend instead. Amma's baby khudos made a better first best friend than he did.

Aadam looked down and began speaking again. "I know—"

"YOU'RE GIVING ME YOUR SPIDERMAN WEBBED-MASTERS WALKIE TALKIE PLATINUM PRO 3000!" I screamed, grabbing the sparkly gadgets from his hands. "No wayyyyyy! Tell me you're lying. Tell me you're lying!"

"Whoa, whoa," Aadam took the walkie talkies off me and held them close. "I'm letting you look at them. That's my present – to let you SEE them properly."

"Ohhhhhhh, right." I watched him place them carefully on the table. Everyone in school had been talking about the limited-edition Platinum 3000s, but they had sold out on the first day and cost way more than the money I had in my bank upstairs.

I thought about it for a moment.

"You still want to be in my story?"

Aadam smiled nervously.

"Want to be written down in history for being the best sidekick of all time?"

His smile grew wider and wider.

"Well, Agent Mahmoud, I have a plan," I finished.

HELLO, LIGHT BULB MOMENT #3!

CHAPTER THIRTY

"Okay, let's go through this again," I said, collecting all the Jaffa cakes together and flattening the piece of paper on the table. "This is me." I pointed to a Jaffa cake I had half eaten and pushed it to the corner. "And this is you," I passed Aadam another one that had been broken and put it in the opposite corner. "And this HUGE one is Affa." I put the only Jaffa cake that was still whole in the middle. "Are you listening?"

"Yes." Aadam had his concentrating face on. I could tell because his eyebrows and eyes almost merged into one piece.

"Okay. It's simple. We both have a walkie talkie so we can be expert spies. If we need to contact each other, we ONLY use the walkie talkies.

We can't have enemies (AKA Amma, Nanu and Khala) compromise this mission. You hear me, soldier?"

"Okay… I mean, sir, yes, sir!" Aadam said, standing up straighter. His fingers shot to his forehead in salute. "Communication received! Sir!"

I looked around to see if the coast was clear. Then, after clearing my throat, I began:

"At exactly 17:55 hours, you will take your place behind the sofa by the window, soldier. I will take mine behind this one." I nodded at the sofa behind us. "Then we'll wait until Affa comes for her six o'clock Instagram break. We'll hide until she least suspects us and then we'll pounce! I'll grab her legs and you grab her head – it's quite heavy so be careful."

"What about her arms?"

"Oh yeah." Aadam was a top dog when it came to plan-checking. "You grab her arms with your feet. Then we'll take her out—"

"And put her in the bin!" Aadam finished. He slam-dunked an imaginary basketball and cheered. "Whoooop, whooooop!"

"Exactly," I smiled, nodding like only spy kids did (puffing up my lips and squinting).

"There's one problem though." Aadam peeked through the curtains to make sure nobody was coming.

"We're scared of Affa."

"True, true." I chomped on the Jaffa cake that was meant to be me and thought hard.

"I've got it!" Aadam's spiky hair bounced into the air as he jumped. "We can have an investigation and search for a plan. How about I take the upstairs and you take the downstairs? I look for clues up there and you look for clues down here.

"Okay," This wasn't a bad idea. It was the best one we had so far (and the only one).

"I'll take both walkie talkies with me to be on the safe side and once we find a plan, we can use them." With that, he took the webbed-masters and put them back in his carrier bag.

"So your plan is to look for a plan?" I eyed him suspiciously. I didn't think plans worked like that.

"Exactamundo, Agent Khan," he said, tossing the HUGE Affa Jaffa in his mouth. "Exactamundo." Aadam roly-polyed across the floor, turned his fingers into a gun and blew on the tip. "See you on the other side, soldier. See you on the other side."

Very quickly, he disappeared through the door, taking his walkie talkies with him.

CHAPTER THIRTY-ONE

In the sitting room, I got back into Batboy mode and looked through all my old research from ages ago. I had no choice but to lay low so I looked under all of the cushions, behind the sofa, beside the television, between the legs of things, and inside the drawers of the little table.

These were the things I found:

- Six fuzzy dustballs shaped like stuffed insects

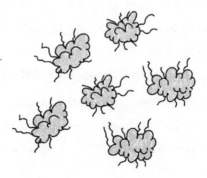

• A paperclip that had been bent into a triangle

• A broken cheese and onion crisp that tasted like mould (yuk)

• A nut – I didn't bother eating that

• The scale of an old fish

I examined the evidence carefully. There had to be a clue in here somewhere. If Aadam was still here, he'd know what to do. I bet he had found a million clues upstairs already.

'AHA! Here it is!' I pulled out a metal tool from between the seats. It snapped like a crocodile and looked like an angry hybrid scissor-chomper. "iLASH - slaying since 2016." I whispered, reading the tiny writing on the handle slowly. I turned the silver weapon in my fingers again. There was more little writing etched into the rim of the scissorhands: 'The devil is in the detail'.

"OH SHUNA MAI-GO!" Could it truly be? So this was what Affa had been hiding all along. It had to be. I, YUSUF ALI KHAN THE FIRST AND LAST, had worked it out: AFFA WAS A TRAINED ASSASSIN. SHE WAS AN ACTUAL TRAINED ASSASSIN. And the worst thing was that she was working with the devil. OOOOOOOOOOHHH Nanu's going to go BANANAS. I can't wait to tell her!

It all made sense now. Her red hair, her control over everyone, the time she nearly killed me with a spear (but failed because I was obviously too HULK for her). And of course, it explained why she was so scared of Nanu. Nanu was ALWAYS reading prayer beads and she smelled of garlicky mothballs. How did I not notice this before? How long had this been going on? When was the last time I had seen her read Qur'an? Of course, the answer was right under my nose.

I sniffed the weapon just to make sure it was hers. It definitely smelled like her − the stench of metallic death tugged at my nostril hairs and almost pulled them clean off. Affa had been slaying people since 2016. By now, she was an expert. Who would be her next victim? Me? Amma? Me? Nanu? Me? Who am I kidding? We all know it's me!

I inspected the chomping-blade again. A red stain was stuck to the top of it. YAA RABB! BLOOD! DRIED BLOOD! Who was her last kill? How long had he been dead for? Why was it on my fingers? IT WAS FRESH! HOLY SNUFF-BALLS, IT WAS FRESH! I was now contaminated. But then I saw it: as clear as day – a rogue eyelash stuck in its teeth. Of course, this was her eyeball squasher. It just had to be. All this time everyone thought that Affa was perfect. Oh boy, oh boy were they wrong.

ARGH! An eyelash! On my wrist! A dead man's actual eyelash! I flung the blade across the room and shook the DNA off me. "GETITOFF GEITTOFF GETITOFF!" I squealed, spinning so fast that I crash-landed onto the sofa and sent all the evidence tumbling down with me.

It was then that a glittering box that wasn't there before revealed itself. It looked at me, daringly like it was telling me to open it even though it wasn't mine. My heart shuddered at the thoughts. What kind of dark magic was this? What kind of evil would I unleash by releasing it?

"Open me," it whispered. "Open meeeeeee."

The voice sounded warm and fuzzy and like home. Who was I to ignore it?

And so, like I was stuck in a trance with no other choice, I unlocked the little chest with a tiny click.

CHAPTER THIRTY-TWO

HOLY JAFFA CAKES!

Inside were the goods: a handgun that could be easily concealed, red ribbon to strangle with, needles and threads to sew eyelids shut once she'd stolen their innards, and … and … could it be? When Affa said she didn't want every Dawud, Mahmood and Ali at her wedding, she wasn't joking! We should have taken her more seriously, but instead we just sat and sipped chaii, pretending everything was alright.

But now in my very fingertips was proof that Affa was a real assassin. Dawud. Mahmood. Ali. They were just some of the names she had crossed out in blood. The red ink on the paper said it all. I hadn't seen any of them since Rabia Affa's wedding last summer. It all made sense now. Dawud Bhai used to be so good to me too. I miss him so much. Not a day goes by that I don't think about him. Once he gave me Affa's samosa when she was saying salaam to everyone – of course, I should have known. The chicken samosa was enough of a reason to take someone out. Wait, what was this? Surely it was a hit list: Affa's own personal hit list and A HIT LIST WITH MY FINGERPRINTS ON IT!

I threw the paper on the floor. There was no way I was going down with her. No way! I had to tell somebody. The police, Nanu, someone! ANYONE! Somebody had to put a stop to this madness.

I was having a nightmare. I was living a real life nightmare. This couldn't be happening. Wake up, Yusuf. Wake up. WAKE UP RIGHT NOW!

Breathe, Yusuf. Breathe. Think straight. Think straight.

There was no question about it, there was definitely more to this FBI investigation than the eye could see. I took a huge, deep breath (x10) and activated stealth mode. Yusuf Ali Khan, spy-detective, would not go down without a fight.

Breathe, Yusuf. Breeeeeeeeeeeeeaaaaaaaaaaaaathe. I scanned the room again, zooming in on Affa's things. The more and more I looked, the more this whole room turned into a crime scene.

And there, in the corner of the room, the most evil of evils: Affa's scarf was hanging on the door handle like some sort of threatening ghost. I should have trusted my gut and destroyed them all when I had the chance.

She had marked her territory and I was on enemy tur-

"What was that?" There was a quiet shuffle. I definitely heard it. "Who's there?" I called out bravely, but it came out as a tiny squeak. "Hello?" I shouted (or at least I thought I did). But nobody answered back. Nobody at all. "Aadam?" But he was supposed to be upstairs and I hadn't heard his elephant footsteps make their way back down again.

I moved towards the door where Affa's scarf hung. There it was again. **SHUFF-SHUFF-SHUFFLE SHUFF-SHUFF-SHUFFLE**.

I froze. So did the noise. Was it following me? What clever tricks were being played here? I was all alone, wasn't I?

WASN'T I?

Taking another step forward, I—

'OH NO!." The shriek escaped from my lips before I could stop it fast enough. I fell to my knees, cradling the little Jaffa cake under my slipper. It must have smushed when I was busy investigating. The chocolatey goodness had splattered all across the paper we had planned our big plans on. "It's okay, baba. It's okay. I'll save you."

I tried picking at what was left of the chocolate, but then my insides nearly exploded. Flapping my ears to turn on supersonic sound mode, I listened again. Even though my heart was trying to launch itself outside of my body, I could still hear it. I ate the Jaffa cake in sheer terror and almost nibbled my fingers off entirely. The shuffle-monster was still at large, and it was louder and closer than ever before. He had come back with a vengeance, and this time he was taking no prisoners.

GULP!

CHAPTER THIRTY-THREE

I quickly crawled behind the sofa. As my hands and butt cheeks were being stabbed by Affa's death traps at every single turn, eyelashes stuck to my arms like leeches. I was a goner; if the monster didn't kill me, then Affa's home-made making-a-murderer kit would!

The shuffle was getting louder and louder. It sounded like an alien with toothbrushes for legs. My heart started thumping quickly. It drop-kicked itself in places I was pretty sure it didn't belong. It was so loud that Ms Hayley's shih tzu could probably hear it from the kennel house next to our school.

"Shhhhhhhhhhhh! Why are you selling me out?" I whispered, poking the place where my heart should have sat still. "WHAT HAVE I DONE TO YOU?"

But the shuffle stopped. It couldn't be far now. It must have been on the other side of the door. I backed up into the tightest corner and squeezed my eyes shut.

Just then, the door clicked open.

Pulling my knees closer, I ducked my head into my hands. Whatever was out there, it was coming for me. And worst of all, I was trapped.

The brush-steps got closer. It would only be a matter of time until the alien discovered me. I was a dead man. I was sure of it.

"Eesoof?"

"AHHHHHHHHHHHHHHHHHHHHHHH!!"

I screamed, jumping up. "I don't wanna die I don't wanna die I don't want to die, Nanu! I don't wanna— Ouch!"

Nanu **THWACKED** me with her broom. "What's the matter with you, boy? Are you trying to give me a heart attack?" An explosion of scarlet gwa-fan juice shot out of her mouth and landed on my lips.

DISGUSTING! GROSS! GROSS! GROSS!

"Oh, it's just you." I managed to say while trying to swallow my sick. Was Nanu ACTUALLY trying to give ME a heart attack? No way was I nuts enough to say that out loud when she had her jedi-master staff with her.

"Who did you think it'd be? Your Abbu?" She had appeared out of nowhere, slowly, slowly brushing the floor. "What did you think I'd do? Kill you? Silly boy..."

So it wasn't an alien-monster after all.

See, I knew there was nothing to worry about.

But all of a sudden, Nanu began to stiffen and her eyes locked in on mine. "Eesoof," she said slowly. Her scarf fell from her head all by itself.

Oh no, maybe she had been taken over by aliens after all!

"You're going to die." Nanu whispered. "I promise you. You will die."

I backed up into the corner again and **GULPED.** What had the aliens done to Nanu?

"Every soul shall taste death," she breathed. Nanu reached for her scarf again. "It's in the Qur'an," she added brightly. "Look it up, young hafidh." With that, she continued sweeping, brushing my feet, my arms and my cheeks so all the leeches and the weapons slid off me.

Who was I kidding? Like an alien would win a fight with Nanu. She'd batter it with her walking stick and leave it for dead. She might not have looked like it, but Nanu was a black-belt ninja.

"Call your Affa and tell her to tidy her craft box, Eesoof." Nanu swept. "Or I'll deep fry her."

"You don't need to tell me twice," I said, collecting the little needles. Craft box - how crafty indeed. "Where are they, by the way?" The house was suspiciously quiet.

Maybe they were planning a surprise party for me.

"In the kitchen, cooking." Nanu said, trying to brush my feet again. "Your sister is doing the Quick Curry Challenge. The perfect wife must know how to put something delicious together very quickly."

And there it was: **DING! DING! DING!**

HELLLOOOOOO, LIGHT BULB MOMENT #4!

CHAPTER THIRTY-FOUR

I had to whisper carefully so Affa wouldn't notice me. "The eagle has been planted," I muttered into the webbed-master from underneath the kitchen table. "I repeat, the eagle has been planted. Over."

"Copy that." Aadam's voice quietly shhhhed through the speakers. I turned the volume down and scanned our infiltrated territory. The top window was cracked open (a good escape route). The curry powders were out (only the chilli would be an epic spy weapon). And the kitchen fan was on (perfect for masking the noise of mine and Aadam's radio intelligence).

After Nanu had left the sitting room, I filled Aadam in on the new plan. He had managed to sneak me into the danger zone undetected by hurling himself down the stairs. There was a HUGE **THUMP** that sounded like it really hurt. Aadam was such a skilled actor that when he cried, I almost thought it was real. Khala was right; he truly was a young Amitabh Bachchan in the making.

I was now staring at Affa through the chair legs. You know what they say, keep your friends close and your enemies closer.

"No! Amma, you go," Affa piped up while stirring the onions. "Two curries is nothing and the other one will take five minutes. Who knows when I'll next get to cook something for you? Plus I've written down the recipe here." Affa put the little piece of paper in her hand down and attacked the pan with her wooden spoon, scrubbing it like she sometimes scrubbed the toilet seat after Aadam's dad used it. She only ever did that if it was starting to burn- the curry (not the toilet).

"Batboy receiving," Aadam whispered again. "Over." The webbed-master shook in my hands.

"Receiving, Captain Underpants," I replied. "Go ahead. Over."

"Yusuf! I'm Spider-bhai now. I told you!" His voice buzzed a little through the speakers.

"Sorry, Spider-bhai." He had chosen so many names that it was hard to keep up. Can you blame me? "What's the 411, oh webbed one?"

This is a super-spy word for intelligence, I think. I don't know for sure, but Affa used to say it all the time when she used to go to school in the Stone Age.

I had to keep a close eye on Amma and Affa as they moved about the kitchen. This was risky business. I tucked the chairs under extra tightly just to make sure that my feet weren't seen. To be on the extra safe side, I sneakily took the ketchup and sriracha sauce from the tabletop and put them on the seat so my head wouldn't peep out. This spy stuff was very tricky indeed.

"No, beti." Amma said, trying to take the wooden spoon off her. She almost whacked Affa with her chunky bangles. Affa dodged it just in time. Come on, FIGHT! FIGHT! FIGHT! "You go. It won't take much longer."

Like always, Amma lost (there was no fight) and Affa sent her out of the kitchen.

"Hawk-eye is here!" Aadam buzzed. Amma must have made it safely onto the other side. "Be careful, Batboy. The fate of the world rests in your hands. No pressure. Over."

Yusuf Ali Khan, amazing spy-superhero, you can do this. This is your time to shine.

Affa clicked through her phone as she stirred and then moved from one side of the kitchen to the other, opening the fridge and the cupboards over and over again. What was she looking for?

FOCUS, YUSUF. FOCUS! How could I get Affa out of the kitchen? She was now getting out spices and sprinkling them into the pan. She started with the yellow one and then the red one. I needed to think quickly. If I knew one thing about cooking (and I didn't know much), it was that the spices were EVERYTHING.

THINK, YUSUF, THINK! She was moving so much that I had to spy between the sauces to avoid detection. WHOOOAAAAAAAA. No way! A mini-mushroom explosion of steam puffed out of the pan after Affa poured a little water into it. Maybe she'd ruin it all by herself.

But I had to be sure. It was too late in the game to leave it up to fate. Suddenly, Affa got her phone and walked towards the table. Oh no! NO NO NO NO! SHE WAS COMING. My cover would be compromised! I REPEAT: MY COVER WOULD BE COMPROMISED!

I needed a plan, but my brain wasn't whirring fast enough. I swiped the sauces off the chair seat and hugged them tightly just as Affa pulled out the chair to sit on it. PHEW!

But I was still in the danger zone. Affa had crossed her legs and her toes were less than a centimetre away from my face. Oh man! Worse still, Affa was swinging her feet too. Her slipper had already fallen off and if I wasn't careful, I was sure I'd find her foot in my face or even worse: her toes up my nose!

This Batman needed a plan. This was a sticky situation I needed to escape from. But how? How?

"Houston," I whispered into the speakers. "We have a problem."

"WHA—"

Aadam shouted so loud that Affa's foot actually froze. I snapped the radio off and placed it carefully on the chair beside me. Biting my arm now, I tried not to breathe. One wrong move and Batboy would be Flatboy–

Affa would crush me. No questions asked.

Come on, Yusuf. Think! Think, I tell you. THINK!

And then it hit me (Plan B, I mean – not Affa's foot). The sticky situation hit me with the full force of my Batman brain power and, as it turned out, the answer was already in my hands.

CHAPTER THIRTY-FIVE

Sriracha sauce: the one thing every brown person had in their home. Rabia Affa even carried it in her bag next to tiny sachets of salt like it was some sort of secret potion. Believe me, I've seen her in restaurants looking around like a meerkat, waiting until she thought nobody was looking, and quickly pouring some onto her chicken and chips before slipping the little bottle out of sight. It got her out of every unseasoned food problem in her life.

One time, Nanu didn't have her glasses on and she mixed the sauce up for Vicks! Yes, you heard me right. VICKS! She rubbed it all over her nose and looked like she had dipped her face into a pot of henna for the whole night. It was a good thing Nanu was made in Bangladesh, otherwise that day might have been the end of her.

Today the very same sriracha sauce was my weapon of choice.

Back in the kitchen, it was hard to dodge Affa's foot because it was swinging so wildly. I pretty much glued myself to the wall and thought my thoughts.

If I sauced Affa's entire foot, she'd feel it and we'd plan my funeral the very next second. If I sauced her toenails and carefully avoided skin contact, then she might just think she has some henna on her toes, which won't help me at all. But if I sauced her slipper and quietly rolled the bottle to the side of the table, she might not detect a thing.

And so it was. I carefully stretched my hand, letting my fingers crawl on the floor and silently picked Affa's slipper up. But at that second, Affa stretched her legs and her long toenail (YES, HER FREAKISHLY LONG TOENAIL) just scraped the end of my nose. GROSS! I held both my breath and the slipper for dear life.

Finally, after half a lifetime, Affa relaxed and lowered her legs. I slurped up the drool that I didn't know had fallen from my lips, let out a quiet sigh of relief and peeled my head away from the wall.

Okay, now was the moment of truth: like a ninja, I unscrewed the cap of the sauce and stealthily poured the chilli liquid into the lonely slipper. After emptying the whole bottle just to be on the safe side, I gently tucked the evidence away.

All I had to do now was wait.

But time really had SLOOOOOOOOOOOWED down to a stop and I thought that maybe Affa had forgotten she existed. Maybe she'd taken a nap in the middle of cooking while waiting for the spices to sweat. But just as those very thoughts filled my brain, Affa jumped to her feet and **SQUELCH!**

'What the actual—," Affa squealed. "EEWWWW! That's gross! That's disgusting!" She started jumping up and down, trying to grab tissues from the tabletop.

I tried to melt into the wall for health and safety reasons. I had to put my hands over my mouth to stop myself from laughing out loud too. It was wayyyyy harder than it looked.

"Yusuf!"

HOLY JAFFA CAKES! How did Affa know? Had she seen me? Oh no! No no no. I put my hands in the air to surrender. I was a dead man. A MURDERED DEAD MAN. I knew it. That gun and ribbon would be put into some real good use. Just as I was about to reveal myself, Affa threw her other slipper at me like a low sliding javelin and it smacked me right on the cheek.

WHAT THE ACTUAL FUDGE-CAKES?

Affa had never ever ever in her whole entire existence thrown anything at me, let alone a slipper. What would be next? Boiled kettle water? The pan of onions? Chilli powder?

"Why doesn't he ever put anything in the right place?" she growled.

HOLD ON ONE STINKING MINUTE. I always put stuff in the right – but wait, wait, wait. Why was she talking to me like I wasn't here? Did she even realise that I was under the table? Did she even know I was alive out here?

I peeked my head out from under the table, carefully avoiding the saucy mess, and saw Affa hop unsteadily out of the kitchen.

CHAPTER THIRTY-SIX

My invisible watch told me that, at most, I had exactly eight minutes and 23 seconds to complete my mission so there was absolutely no time to waste. I had to think fast. Last time this happened, I accidentally made the world's best chaii and Affa became a hero in seven and a half minutes flat. This time, she wouldn't be so lucky. Not if I had something to do with it.

I grabbed the magnetic crayon that was stuck to the fridge and snatched the little paper with the recipe on it.

This is what it said:
five crushed garlics
half a big onion
two teaspoons of salt
four pieces of hutki fish
five fish heads
three chopped potatoes
chilli, tumeric and coriander powder
two cups of water
four green chillies

Five crushed garlics. Hmm, what if I made it 10? That would be too obvious. I had to be smarter than that.

I sharpened my teeth on the crayon and thought hard. What could be more realistic? Affa puts garlic in everything – her curries, her snacks, her socks. Something that looked like it could trick her. But what?

I inspected the kitchen quickly. Aha! The apple. Like a huge hungry caterpillar, I chomp-chomp-chomped, spitting out five little chunks of apple. I quickly peeled the skin with my teeth and lay double-agent garlic disguises onto the table. This plan was fool-proof.

Okay, next: half a big onion. I could get a scoop of ice cream. No, that would make it nicer. No more Mr Nice Guy, remember? I looked at the clock on the oven. Six minutes and 32 seconds! BUT WHERE HAD THE TIME GONE? Think faster, think faster.

The cricket ball! Of course! Why didn't I think of that before? I scribbled it down quickly.

Next: two teaspoons of salt to two teaspoons of flour. Simple.

The hutki pieces and fish heads were disgusting enough. Better keep those in. I added an extra helpful note beside it: keep the juicy eyeballs and boil them until they explode.

Three chopped potatoes turned into three chopped toes – all I had to do was cross out the 'pota'.

This was a lot easier than I thought it would be.

2 cups of toilet water – that should do it.

The chilies, the chilies...

I dove into the cupboards, searching for the best swap possible. I rattled through the lentil jars, pepper balls, the rice flour and elasies (I definitely wasn't making that mistake again). Yes! African ghost chillies! We have African ghost chillies! Affa must have bought some new ones. There were only six. I couldn't use all of them. It would look too obvious. And I didn't want Nanu to turn into a ghost either. She was scary enough already.

I grabbed the crayon and turned '4 green' chillies to '4 ghost' chillies and added a top tip too: add the reddest, most devil-looking, evil ones.

This was perfect. Absolutely perfect. Say goodbye to Masterchef, Affa. Say goodbye, my friend.

A quick time-check told me I had two minutes and 84 seconds left, but there were apple peels on the floor, pepper balls all over the table and an explosion of lentils scattered across the kitchen. When did this happen? More importantly, who did this? Did Aadam sneak in while I had my back to the door?

"Ammaaaaaaaaaaaaaa," Affa shrieked from upstairs. "Can you check on the curry?"

Suddenly, the webbed-master flashed bright red and buzzed back to life. "INCOMING!" Aadam screamed through the speakers. "HAWK-EYE IS ON THE LOOSE! I REPEAT, HAWK-EYE IS ON THE LOOSE! Inna-lillahi wa inna ilayhi rajioon!"

You only ever really say this when somebody dies! It means 'To God we belong and to God we will return', but I'm not ready to return now!

"FIND COVER RIGHT NOW," Aadam squeaked. "OR PREPARE TO DIE!"

156

CHAPTER THIRTY-SEVEN

I snatched the walkie-talkie from the chair, slammed the kitchen door shut, and used the exact same chair to barricade the door. Nobody was getting in. Or out. Not on my watch.

"Aadam!" I yelled, shaking the speakers. "I need more time. Buy me more time!"

"You got it, sir," he snapped straight back. "Leave it to me."

I threw the webbed-master onto the table just as a high-pitched howl echoed through the house. There was a huge thunder rumble from upstairs and the ceiling shook above me.

Was that— No, Yusuf! Focus.

Grabbing the pepper pot, I scooped up all the black little balls I could. But some of them escaped and ran loops around the cupboards. The ones that had escaped for freedom looked like ginormous ants bolting for the back door.

"Come back!" I shouted. "Why aren't you listening to me? Come back!" I shot after them, rolling them into the pot on the way. The last one sprinted towards the sink, avoiding all the obstacles in its path. It slipped over the knife, scuttled across the chopping board and made a beeline for the drippy tap. It rolled faster and faster and further and further until…"Aha! I got you."

But it crawled "out of hands" like an expert bowling ball.

Wait, what? IT WAS AN ANT? I had been chasing ants! No wonder it was rolling away so fast – poor guy was running for his life! I peeked inside the little glass pot. Phew, there were only two creepy crawlies in there. I shook them out on to the floor and slid the pepper pot back into the cupboard.

Next: the lentils. It was like a minefield. I had to be careful. One wrong move and the whole thing would… I didn't know what it would actually do, but it would be a disaster. I was 98.7% sure of it.

I grabbed the vase from the windowsill and plucked the flowers out of it, throwing them into the brown bin. Zooming across the whole kitchen like a witch on a broomstick, I shooed every single lentil back in until there was absolutely none left.

"Good work, Bat—" Oh no! The apple peels. I dove for them just as the door handle rattled. Somebody was on the other side desperate to get in. Come on come on come on. I snatched the peels as the chair that held the kitchen door shut flew across the kitchen.

A rogue apple skin caught my foot and I went flying into the air.

"NOOOOOOOOOOOOOOOOOOOOOOO!"

The peels soared skywards, and I grabbed onto the cupboard door for dear life. My hand slipped and tore right through a paper packet, making the rice flour erupt like hot lava and rain all over me.

SLAP!

The apple peel had come back down to Earth and landed on my nose.

"AAAARRRRGGGGGGHHHHHHH, A GHOST!"

Aadam squealed, pointing with a threatening finger. His nose was bleeding and he had a swollen eye. "There is no God but Allah, there is no God but Allah!"

"WHAT? Where's the booth?

Yep, you got it – a 'booth' is a ghost.

Where's the b —" I grabbed the steel bowl and a TERRIFYING CLOWN stared back at- "Oh, It's just me, doofus." I shouted, brushing the ghost-dust off me.

"Oh," he said, spotting his webbed master on the table. "I knew that."

"Come on! Help me up before Amma comes."

But Aadam had already turned towards the door, staring with horror at something behind it. "Too late," he squeaked just as Hawk-eye reared her ~~ugly~~ head.

CHAPTER THIRTY-EIGHT

"And then, Amma," I explained while eating another scoop of rice and dhaal, "the flour just fell on me, just like that. I didn't even touch it at all. It just threw itself on me while I was minding my own business and doing absolutely nothing wrong." I sucked the dhaal off my fingers one at a time.

Amma nodded while nibbling on a chicken bone. Affa and Nanu were eating around the kitchen table too. The rice was steaming and the fresh smell of our curries tickled my nose-buds.

It was just the four of us again. Khala had said that Aadam had 'one too many adventures' today and dragged him home without the webbed-masters. I made a secret plan to play with them later and even bribe Nanu with gwa-faan so she could be a spy too.

"I see," Amma said, staring at me, staring right through me, glaring directly into my soul so my bones shook my very insides.

Affa and Nanu were in on it too. They just waited for me to speak, to tell the truth, to spill the beans, to confess what truly happened. No way was I doing that. My lips were sealed, locked tight and I had thrown away the key already. I wasn't backing down now. Not in a million years, not even if they tortured me to the very en-

"IT WAS ME!"

Who said that? WHO SAID THAT? Who on the whole of planet Earth, the sun, the stars and the galaxies beyond said that?

"What was you, Yusuf?" Affa said, helping herself to more rice. The metal spoon clinked against the pan.

Not again. "What was me?" I groaned, stuffing a whole mound of rice into my mouth and piling it so much that if I spoke properly, the whole thing would explode. "DOIBLOB BLOOOMBUTT HUMMMMBUG SAAAAAAA." FYI: this doesn't mean anything.

162

There. that should throw them off the scent.

"Don't talk with your mouthful, baba." Amma drank her glass of water slowly.

"OKAY, okay. You got me, Inspector Amma. I'll confess. Just stop pressuring me!" I wiped the sweat juices on my forehead away, but it just felt even stickier than before because I used the wrong hand.

Amma, Affa and Nanu looked at each other without blinking. They were plotting already. I could see right through them. Yusuf Ali Khan was no fool. No way was he.

And just like that, the truth, the whole truth and nothing but the truth came tumbling out of my mouth like quick sick.

"So Nanu," I finally finished, licking my teeth clean. "It's only a little bit of toilet water you're drinking. I made sure Affa only used two cups. Nothing more, nothing less. You can thank me later." I winked (or maybe it was a twitch). Webbed-masters Pro3000, here I come. I sighed gladly. "I'm glad I got that off my chest. Telling the truth with no punishment feels much better. Thanks, Ammu-jan. You're the best!"

Amma raised her eyebrows and Nanu's face began to scrunch up. Steam (from her nose? From the rice? From the curry? From her angry-looking skin? God knows) clouded her googly spectacles.

But Affa just burst out laughing and spat the fish head she was sucking straight out of her mouth. It shot across the table and plopped directly onto my plate. GROSS.

"But this is the best hutki I've ever had in my whole entire life," Nanu began, wiggling a dead fish in my direction. "You mean to tell me that I'm eating food cooked in toilet water?"

"No, Nanu. Like I'd follow his recipe. I can tell the difference between my pen and a crayon, you know. Plus Yusuf can't spell." Affa chuckled evilly, reaching for her fish head again. "Want some?" she offered.

"I'd rather eat my stinky P.E. socks dipped in armpit, thanks."

"Ewwwww," she whined while chewing the eye sockets. "That's absolutely disgusting."

Oh yeah, I'm the disgusting one. She licked her fingers clean and got up, pulling me to the sink with her. "Jokes on you anyway, Agent Khan," she whispered, scrubbing my forehead so much that it made me all woozy. "That curry Nanu loves?" She checked to make sure no one was looking. "It's a takeaway. Rabia Affa made it."

What the fudge-cakes? Affa had a game plan all along.

Her smile grew wider and wider. "She snuck it in through the back garden about half an hour ago. I should thank you really for creating such a big scene."

Oh, maaaaaaaaaaaaaaaaaan. Not again!

Affa 2: Yusuf 1.

CHAPTER THIRTY-NINE

"Wake up, Yusuf! WAKE UP!"

There was banging on the door and the whole Earth was shaking.

"Whassat? Whooz der?" I pulled the covers over my head, sandwiching myself between the pillows. "Hmmmmmm, warmmmmmmm." Still pitch black. Just a nightmare. Bad dream. I blew on my left shoulder and rolled to my right. "Hmmmmmmmmm, warmmmmmmmmmmmmm."

"Yusuf Ali Khan!" Affa shouted, yanking the door open and letting the light in like lightning. "Get your backside out of bed, sunshine. We're going shopping." She threw the covers on the floor and grabbed my waist, pulling me out of my den.

"No, Affa. NOOOOOOOOOO!" I dug my nails into the mattress, holding on for dear life. "Just a nightmare. Just a nightmare! Audhubillah, audhubillah." I shut my eyes tight to make it all go away.

Affa tells me to say that when

something creeps me out. I guess she doesn't know that I mostly use it against her.

"Stop it!" Affa said, pulling me harder.

Why wasn't it going away?

"We…" she pulled again, activating hulk-mode, "have got…"

My hands were slipping already. FAIL ME NOT, HANDS. FAIL ME NOT!

"… shopping…"

We both squeezed tighter.

"… to do!" She tugged at my pyjamas so hard that she pulled my pants right off and went flying – CRASH! – into the wardrobe.

Oh, dear.

I grabbed the blanket and rolled myself inside it like a spring roll, but Affa was looking a little woozy AND she still had my pants.

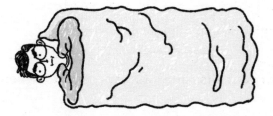

Climbing over her legs and onto her side, I rolled myself beside her and stuffed myself under her armpit. "Hmmmmmmmmmm, warmmmmmmmmm." She actually smelled like Jaffa cakes too. What soap had she used?

"Whassat? Whooz der?" she mumbled. Her eyes were all droopy. Affa definitely needed some more sleep. "Yusuf?" she whispered, sniffing my hair sleepily. "I'm going to kill you one day. You know that?"

"Hmmmmmmmmmmm, warmmmmmmmmmm."

But then I remembered the red hair, the gun, the craft box, THE HIT LIST, and my eyes flew right open. Maybe Nanu was wrong. Maybe it wasn't the guest list after all. Maybe she really was an assassin at heart.

And here I was, half-asleep and stuffed under her arm. If I wasn't careful, she'd snake-mode strangle me in my sleep.

"AFFFFFFFFFFAAAAAAA!" I yelled in her ear, making her jump out of her skin. "WHAT ARE YOU DOING? WE GOTS SOME SHOPPING TO DO!"

CHAPTER FORTY

"Affa, why are you spending £200 on burgers and chips?"
I asked her, sneaking some Kinder Surprises, tomato
ketchup crisps, gulab jamun, rasmalai, guava and fish
fingers in the trolley. I waited for her to finish checking
for the halal sign and inspect another row of jackfruit
before slipping it under the frozen goods. "I can't eat all
of that by myself, can I?" Or could I? "Well, at least not
in one go."

Affa paused at the fruit section, sniffing the sweet mangoes beside the papaya. "I want a burger bar for the mehndi." She got her phone out and tapped at her list. "I think that's everything, you know."

"Finally," I breathed. "This trolley is JAAAAAAAAM-PACKED." Even the cucumbers were threatening to roll right off the sides.

"Well, we could take out all the rubbish you've snuck in there."

"YOU SAW THAT?" But I was in super-spy mode! How could my powers have failed me?

"Bro, I invented that. Oh wait! Excuse me," Affa waved at a worker to get his attention. He was soooooo tall – almost like Groot (grown-up Groot, of course). He actually had to bend a little to hear Affa's quacks.

"Ji?"

This means yes, but it can be both the question or the answer. Don't look at me. I didn't make the rules. I just follow them – kind of. Okay, not really.

The man looked from the trolley to Affa to the trolley again.

"Do you have any ribbon?" she asked. "We need some for the gate, Yusuf. You'll be in charge of that."

"Me?" Yusuf Ali Khan? In charge of something? Affa must have really hit her head hard this morning. "Sir, yes, sir! Ribbon, please." I asked the towering Groot.

He smiled and nodded. "Ji." His blue turban looked super cool with his white jacket. If only he had a claw for a hand, then he could have been a mad scientist. "Come, come."

We wheeled the food trolley through a maze of spices, through walls of pots and pans, through dead chicken guts and lamb flesh, and then finally towards the fish counter.

"Erm, Affa?" I said, glaring hard at a fish eyeball. "Tell it to stop looking at me."

Affa looked just as confused as the fish did.

Groot spoke to another man with black curly hair and a fuzzy caterpillar for a mustache. "Yes?" The caterpillar wiggled.

"We were looking for ribbon," Affa explained again, pulling the trolley closer to her.

"Ji, ji," he nodded. "How can I help?" He took a HUGE frozen fish and nearly shoved it down Affa's throat. "Want some? The best in the city."

"No, no, no," Affa said, waving the great tail away. Groot-man looked at us funny. "We just want ribbon."

Groot nodded again. "Ji, ji."

I scratched my head. "How can a human being be a ribbon?"

Something definitely smelled fishy here. And I wasn't talking about the zombie baby sharks and fish guts either.

"I am Ripon," the other man smiled. "What about fish eggs? You like fish eggs?"

"Ribbon," Affa laughed. "R-I-B-B-O-N." But the whole trolley shook. One more move and there'd be a tsunami of fish fingers.

"Fish fingers!" Of course. "No wonder the fish were staring at me funny. They know we're going to be frying all their pals. Fish are food, you hear me? Not friends." I looked the beast straight in the googly eye and poked the glass. "You hear me?"

"You're so weird," Affa said, waving goodbye to the mustache and Groot..

"I know you are, but what am I?" I turned back to the worker-men. "I guess we must-dash! Like mustache, get it? Get it?"

CHAPTER FORTY-ONE

"You're up to something, Yusuf Ali Khan," Affa said, nibbling on a chicken bone. The crumbly bits stuck to Affa's scarf. She always liked to save her food there for later. Sometimes, if I was lucky, I'd find it first.

"You can't prove nuthin', soldier," I said, shaking my head. "Nuthin', you hear me? Nada."

We were in Krispy Fried Chicken, the best chicken shop in town. They had ginormous windows that let you see right through the glass of the arcade on the other side of the street, and wide, puffy blue and red seats that made you feel like Captain America. Better still, for £2.99, Affa could get me flaming popcorn chicken bites, two crispy chicken wings, some chips with ketchup and a Fruit Shoot. Every time I came here, I felt like a king – a chicken wing king.

"Hmmm, we'll see about that, young hobbit." Affa took another bite of her stinger burger. The saucy goodness escaped from her mouth and almost fell onto the table, but I caught it just in time with my finger and stuck it to my chip. "Ewwwww, that's disgusting."

She scrunched up her face. For a second, I thought she had turned into Nanu! "That's literally been in my mouth."

I licked the sauce off first and chomped the chip up afterwards. "Affa, please. This dripped from your face, not mine. Who's really the gross one here?"

She laughed, almost choking on her mouthful, and looked at me like I was ill.

I felt my forehead with my chip-free hand. Nope, no ills here. Not yet, anyway.

"I'm going to miss this, you know. It's really sad."

"What do you mean?" Was Affa never going to take me out anymore?

"Yusuf, Manchester is over two hours away. You do know that, right?"

"Yeah, we went last month. Remember?" Did she not remember that I had supersonic memory skills? We actually made the mistake of taking Aadam with us that day and he was sick all over the seat. Two hours really does feel like forever when you're cooped up with lumpy stink bomb explosions.

"Exactly. I won't be here as much, will I? But when I am here, I'll make it extra special. Promise."

HOLD ON ONE STINKING MINUTE. "Wait, am I hearing this right?"

Affa stroked my cheek. "I mean, I'll always be your sister and we'll still see each other—"

"I CAN HAVE YOUR BEDROOM? AFFA! You're the BEST!"

"Hold up, what?" Her fingers froze. "Seriously? Did you even listen to what I said?"

I stole a chip from her plate. Hers were getting cold anyway. "I always listen. You said," I made my voice softer like she did and poked my fingers into her cheek, smearing ketchup with each stroke. "I won't be here as much, will I? But when I am here, I'll make it extra special. Promise."

BOOOOOOOOOOOOM SHAKA-LAKA-LAKA, BOOM! Supersonic memory skills still good!

"God help me," Affa said, stuffing the last of her burger in her face. "And FYI, my room is MINE. Go anywhere near it, you're a dead man. Understood?"

I nodded. We'll see about that, Ms Ultimate Bossy-Pants. We'll see about that.

CHAPTER FORTY-TWO

Time was running out. The wedding was in less than 96 hours and I still had absolutely no plan, no mission and no way to stop Affa's wedding.

Think, Yusuf. Think!

I took another bite of Bombay mix and crunched it as my brain whirred into action. When it was just me and Nanu in the house, Nanu let me eat whatever I wanted, including an entire jar of spicy snacks. Yes, my mouth would burn and I'd spend an extra hour on the toilet seat, but boy, oh boy, was it worth it.

"EEEEEEESOOOOOOOOOOOOOOOF!" Nanu's voice croaked from upstairs.

"NANNUUUUUUUUUUUUUUU?" I called back, almost choking on a chilli lentil.

"I'm having my nap," Nanu yelled. "Your mammi will phone in about five minutes time. Tell her I'll ring her back later. Don't tell her much more. She likes to gossip, that one."

"Okay, Nanu."

Now, normally, FREEEEEEEEEEEEDOM like this was like Golden Time at school. It was the best time to stretch my legs all over the table, starfish on the sofa, and nibble on every sugary thing in our fridge. But there was no time for that today. None at all. All I could do was pace about the room and try to figure out how to stop the biggest party in our family since ever.

No pressure.

"WHAT AM I GOING TO DO?" I whisper-yelled, giving up on the Bombay mix and plopping to the floor. "WHAT HAVE I DONE TO DESERVE THIS?"

BRING-BRIIIIIIIIIIINNNNNNNNG! BRING-BRIIIIIIIIIIINNNNNNNNG!

I guess Nanu wasn't wrong when she said five minutes.

"Hello— I mean, as-salamu 'alaikum."

"Who is this?" Mammi asked. I'd recognise her squeaky voice from a light year off.

Who am I? SHE rang OUR house!

"It's Yusuf, obviously." Honestly, who was she expecting? Shrek?

"Don't be rude," she snapped. "Where's your Nanu?"

"I'm fine, thank you very much for asking. How are you, Mammi?"

"Your Nanu," she repeated. "Where is she?"

I sighed, stopping myself from putting the phone down. You just can't teach anyone manners these days.

"She's napping. She said she'll call you back."

"So how old are you?" Mammi interrupted. She asked this every week. EVERY SINGLE WEEK!

"I'm nine and three-quarters, remember?"

"Hmmmmmmmm, not old enough. How old's your sister? Is she married?"

"Well, she's getting… " I trailed off, remembering what Nanu had said. What if I could use this as part of MY PLAN? If Mammi loves to gossip, well then gossip she will. "She was supposed to get married, but the wedding's been called off!" There, that should do it. This would only be a lie if my plan DIDN'T work. Now I had no choice but to make sure it did!

"No way!" Mammi was getting excited. Her voice had gone even higher pitched if that was even possible.

"Why?" She sounded like she was chewing on something. "Tell me more. I mean, why is my darling niece no longer engaged?"

"Well, uh, she..." Oh man, I didn't think that far ahead. "Well she's been very sick lately. She's been sick a lot! Lots of throwing up, it's all gross and smelly. Um, and ... the doctor said she doesn't have long left!" That should do it! A dying girl would never think of getting married in that state.

"Oh my, oh my!" Mammi said. I could hear her giggling. "What a naughty girl."

Why was she laughing?

"Yes! That's it. She's very naughty!"

Yusuf Ali Khan, you are a genius!

"It's no wonder your mum has been awfully quiet lately. How long has she got left?"

I couldn't say days, that would be too obvious. "Weeks, I think. It's a really difficult time for us and I don't think you should ever call again. I've said too much." **HEHEHEHEHEHEHE.**

"No, Yaqub—"

"It's Yusuf."

179

"Whatever, you said just enough. Goodbye!"

And with that, she hung up.

All I had to do now was wait for her to spread the word.

CHAPTER FORTY-THREE

It turned out that it didn't take very long for Mammi to spread the word. Very soon, the phone was ringing off the hook.

"She's got a flesh-eating disease!" I said to one aunty Okay, maybe this was a teeny tiny white lie, but I had to make sure that I was telling the truth about the wedding being cancelled at ALL COSTS. What choice did I have?

"She did something unspeakable and decided to join the circus to become a mute." I said to another.

"A monkey breathed on her in the zoo last week and now she's going ape!" I repeated to somebody else.

"She had a secret wedding and now she's getting a divorce!" I squealed, sounding just like Mammi.

But it wouldn't stop! The calls kept coming and each time, I had forgotten what I had said in the first place.

Soon the lies were spiralling out of control. I didn't know when I was fibbing and when I was telling the truth. Affa seemed to have gone from being a leper to leaping off a building in fifteen minutes flat. I almost believed she had crushed every single bone in her body and was now lying in a hospital bed being operated on by an MI5 special doctor who was known for eating people's lungs! (Poor Affa! She needed those to breathe.)

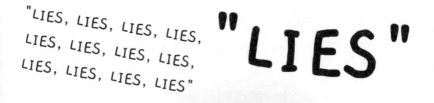

By the time Nanu's door creaked again, I must have taken 3.7 million calls. One thing for sure was that everybody knew that the wedding was off. My job here was done.

BRING-BRIIIIIIIIIIINNNNNNNNG! BRING-BRIIIIIIIIIIINNNNNNNNG!

SHOWTIME!

I answered the phone, pretending to cry.

"WAAAAHHHH WAAAAAAAAAAH WAAAAAAAAH," I added a hiccup for good measure. "She's gone. Affa's gone. It happened so quickly. God just loved her too much and she was too good for this world."

Amibabh Bachchan, watch out!

"YUSUF ALI KHAN!"

I froze.

Amma's voice echoed through the phone again as my fingers trembled.

"Open the front door."

CHAPTER FORTY-FOUR

"Mum told me you're going through a lot right now and that's why you told all those lies. She says you're attention-seeking because you don't know how to cope," Aadam said, patting me on the back. He put a big yellow bag on the sitting room table. He had separated it from all the trays of henna cones and snacks Khala had brought in with her. "She and Khala spent all day yesterday saying sorry to everyone. I'm surprised you're not dead."

"Yeah, me too. Amma said she'd deal with me after damage control - whatever that means. She made me promise not to tell Affa anything either." I tried to sneak a peek inside. "I wonder what I'm going through."

Maybe parasites had taken over my body, or even a caterpillar I didn't know about was stuck in my nose and had built a nest.

"Yeah. I wonder too." He ruffled the bag, but it didn't move. Whatever was inside it had to be pretty big.

"So I got you something to make you feel better."

"YOU DID?" I could feel my eyelids peeling back, making my eyeballs almost pop out. Keep it cool, Yusuf. Keep it cool. "I mean, yes, I'm going through lots. Lots, lots, lots." I rolled one of the henna cones that Khala left on the table, but it was no use. My eyes were stuck to the great bag of mysteries.

"I knew it." He nodded, dipping his hands inside it.

Play it cool, Yusuf.

"WHATISIT? WHATISIT? WHATISIT?"

Who said that? WHO SAID THAT?

"Mum said you have to be strong."

"I do, I do." JUST OPEN THE BAG, AADAM! OPEN IT NOW!

"I know, so I got you this to help you." He slowly, slowly, like he was an extra slow tortoise, reached inside the bag. His fingers stayed there for AGES before he lifted them higher, dragging out. NO WAY! TELL ME I'M DREAMING. TELL ME I'M DREAMING.

"Your Hulk Smash Hands boxing gloves!" I dove for them but stopped mid-air. "Wait, are you letting me just look at them or can I touch them too?"

He scrunched up the bag. "Nope, they're all yours. To keep, to touch, to do whatever. They're 100% yours."

No way! "Aadam, you're the best!" I grabbed them and stuffed my hands inside. Now I could really activate Hulk mode. "Are you sure?"

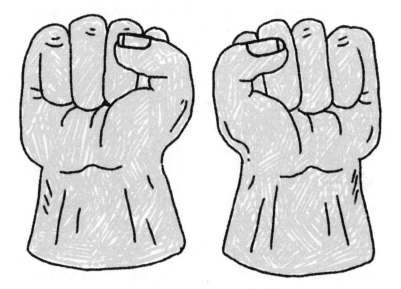

Why did I ask? Why did I ask? Why did I ask?

"Yep," he smiled, taking his webbed-masters walkie talkies from the shelf – when did they get there? I thought I'd hid them. "They're 300% yours."

"Yes!" I punched the air. So much power. AND IT'S ALL MINE!

"They're all yours — for the next ten minutes, anyway. Then please give them back."

"WHAT?" I raised my eyebrows.

"I'm just messing with you! They're yours forever."

Aadam passed me a walkie talkie to balance on my monster fists. Pushing me behind the sofa, he switched it on and disappeared.

"Talk to me, Batboy." The webbed-masters buzzed. "What's happening? Over."

I sighed and took the Hulk Smash Hands off. Aadam wouldn't understand. "You know, we won't have a man of the house anymore. They're taking ours to Manchester where all the men end up. The clue is in the name. What are we going to do? Over."

"Can you not just be the man? It's got to be easier than all this plotting. I can help you. We could be a team. Dad does it all the time and he makes it look so easy."

See? I knew he wouldn't get it. He wouldn't have to be one. "It's not easy for Affa. She does everything; the house, the food, taking care of Nanu. She gets me Jaffa Cakes, and tells me all the things that Sheikh Google won't.

Before all this wedding stuff, she used to play football with me, and cricket, and wrestling, and... everything. You don't get it." He wouldn't ever get it. He didn't know how hard it had been for us.

My breathing started getting funny, but I didn't think an inhaler would help this time.

Keep it cool, Yusuf. Keep it cool.

"Affa keeps Amma happy. And Amma gets sad when she's not here. When Amma's angry, it's okay. But when she's sad, she's sad for a long time." I pulled the web-masters closer. "How is that fair, Aadam? Why should she have to go? Why can't Umar Bhai come live with us? Why is he taking her away? Why do that to us? She's been my sister longer than he was anything to her!" Now that I was all wobbly, I tried to steady myself and breathe properly again. "I mean," I said, starting again. "You have your Dad - we... we just don't. It's - it's," I didn't know what else to say, but, "over."

Aadam didn't say anything either. Maybe the battery stopped working. Just as I was about to poke my head out from behind the sofa, the webbed-masters buzzed back to life.

"Agent Khan," Aadam whispered. "I have a plan."

CHAPTER FORTY-FIVE

"Okay," Aadam said, double, triple, quadruple checking the door was shut and that there were no flies on the walls. There was one moth, but as long as it stayed in the corner of the ceiling, we were a-okay. "Drastic times call for desperate measures. You gets me?"

In cool language, this means 'do you understand?' I'm a fast learner.

No. I didn't. But it sounded cool so I nodded, trying not to give anything away.

"You tell me, Agent Khan," he pulled the table closer to us and wiggled his butt deeper into the sofa. "What is the SINGLE most important thing at a wedding?"

Easy. "The food." Hold on, were we going to poison people?

He shook his head. "The next most important thing."

"The cake." Could we really plot the greatest cake heist in living memory?

"The next most important thing."

"The balloons…"

"No, Yusuf! Think again. What is THE most important thing? What can't you do without?"

This was obviously not a good time to tell Aadam that you really couldn't complete a wedding without food, cakes and balloons. There had to be something else.

"Oh, I know." Duh. How had I not thought of it before? "Two people that actually want to spend infinity and beyond living in the same house together and want to try their best to love each other." Boom! Two reward points to me!

"No!" Aadam was actually glowing pink. I didn't even know that was possible. "You don't need that."

"Of course you do, Aadam." I might not know much, but I knew that much. "I'm 207% sure you need that. It goes food, cake, two people who—"

"A DRESS!" He screamed, jumping up and down. "YOU NEED A WEDDING DRESS!"

"Aadam Mahmoud," I tried to unclamp his hands from my shoulders. For a skinny boy, he was freakishly strong. Like Wolverine, Aadam probably had Aadam-man-tium in his bones. Maybe he would grow up to be a man after all. "You are a genius. We can hide the dress in the recycle bin. Affa won't have time to buy a new one. It took them months to make this one."

But Aadam wasn't listening. His eyes had gone all woozy and he wasn't looking at me anymore. In fact, I didn't even think that he was on this planet anymore.

"Aadam? Aaaaaadaaaaaam?" I clapped my hands in front of his face, but nothing. "AGENT MAHMOUD, report to headquarters. Agent... agent..."

But his soul had already gone. What was left of the real Aadam had just disappeared. All that remained was just his body, standing still and just staring into space. I shook him hard. "DON'T LEAVE MEEEEEEE.-"

"Yusuf," he whispered. His eyes stopped being glassy and he snapped back to normal. Thank God. He picked up a henna cone from the table behind me and rolled it between his fingers. A huge smile splattered across his face and something told me that the Joker himself had possessed him.

"I," he said, looking up boldly, "have a better plan."

CHAPTER FORTY-SIX

Aadam's eyebrows twitched and he tapped the tips of his fingers together. "Number two," he whispered, rocking back and forth. "Number two. Number two."

"That's not a better plan," I snapped. Had the Aadam-man-tium meddled with his brain? Did I need to put HIM in the bin? "I repeat, Aadam: that is NOT a better plan."

"Of course, it is!" he jumped up and down. "It's absolutely perfect. Nobody in their right mind would wear a dress covered in brown goo." He lowered his voice to make sure absolutely no one could hear us. "It looks like a, you know... a number two. It looks like goo."

HE'S TALKING ABOUT POOOOOOOOOO!

We pressed our ears against Affa's bedroom door - WAIT! HOLD ON! WHAT JUST HAPPENED? HOW ON THE WHOLE OF PLANET EARTH, THE SUN,

THE STARS AND THE GALAXIES BEYOND DID WE GET TO AFFA'S BEDROOM? When did that happen? Did I blackout? Or did I black-in? Did a black hole just suck me up and spit me out here?

Wait a minute! I'd just figured out Aadam's superpower: TELEPORTATION.

"Come on, let's go."

Without warning, Aadam grabbed my arm and vortexed me into Affa's lair. I didn't even have time to argue.

GULP!

There it was: the wedding dress, hanging or should I say weighing down Affa's door.

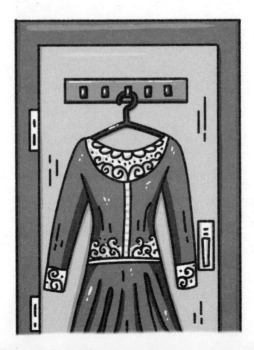

"Woaaaaaaaaaah," Aadam breathed.

Woaaaaaaaaaaaaaaaaah, indeed.

Before us was the glittering beast. It looked like Iron Man's suit had crash-landed into a Christmas tree and had exploded into Affa's dress. The gold chainmail and red armour would definitely protect her from any arrows, gunfire and any aunties that tried to get in her way.

I twisted the henna cone in my hand like a knife. WHEN DID THAT GET THERE? WHO DID THIS? WHAT WAS HAPPENING TO ME?

Aadam held one too, pulling it out from his pocket. "Come on, Yusuf. Let's do this." His voice was shaking. "You go first." That wasn't just Aadam talking, it was Fear, and Fear itself was holding him back.

"No, you go first. You're the man with the plan." No way was I starting. Nope. No way. Never.

"She's YOUR sister," he said, lifting his dagger henna cone to my neck and pushing me closer to the dress. "You can do this. No. You WILL do this."

But something told me I wouldn't. The whole thing was so heavy that with one wrong move, it could all fall down, knock me clean out and alert the whole house like a huge NEENAW signal. "I don't think I can. You've put your faith in the wrong man, soldier."

"No, never! Agent Khan, you can do this. Remember why you're doing it. Remember who the real enemy is." His voice had stopped shaking and he turned to me instead, aiming the cone at my heart. Right now, with the cone of death millimetres away from me, it was hard to tell who the real enemy actually was.

But Aadam was right. Without this sparkly monster, there would be no wedding. It was the key to everything: my hopes, my dreams and MY FAMILY. I was doing this for them.

I closed my eyes and breathed deeply. "For Nanu," I whispered, taking a step forward. "For Amma." I continued like a little prayer. The henna cone was heavy in my hand. I pressed it carefully, keeping my finger on the tip so it wouldn't drip on to the white carpet.

"Affa's coming!" Aadam squeaked, pulling me away from the dress and diving headfirst under the bed.

The footsteps were getting louder and louder and faster and faster and closer and closer. She was coming. Worse still, she wasn't alone!

I jumped into Affa's wardrobe at lightning speed, put my hand over my mouth and held my breath just as Affa and Khala spilled into the room.

CHAPTER FORTY-SEVEN

The bed creaked heavily, and the wardrobe door jammed shut. This meant that somebody was on the other side of this very door and that someone else was sitting on top of Aadam!

If we were caught, we'd be mincemeat and Affa would mince us herself. I didn't like the sound of that.

The door moaned again and I hid deeper and deeper into Affa's jungle of dresses. It would have been easier if it wasn't so dark and if her clothes didn't feel like a million spiders crawling up my arms, ears and neck. Gross. Gross gross gross.

"I don't know, Khala," Affa's voice boomed against the door, making both me and it shudder. IT WAS HER! She was there. Affa was on the other side! "I just worry about them. I can't help it."

"I know you do, but all that worrying will get you nowhere." I pictured Khala swinging her legs, imagining she kicked Aadam's face by accident. If that happened, we'd both be goners because when Aadam got in trouble, he took everybody down with him, even Ms Hayley's shih tzu. Trust me, I've witnessed it firsthand.

"I knew you were going to say that. It's just… it's just," AND THEN SHE OPENED THE WARDROBE DOOR. HOLY SNOTBALLS, SHE OPENED THE WARDROBE DOOR, letting half the light in. I froze. One move – one wrong move – and that was it. Affa's floating hand rummaged through her scarves. I super-glued myself to the wall, trying to melt into it, but it was closing in on me. I REPEAT: IT WAS CLOSING IN ON ME. Ya Rabb, put a stop to this madness! Please.

But Affa's arm wiggled like a snake searching for its prey. The mighty python slithered towards my pocket. Wait for it… wait for it… oh no! Its fangs snapped and snapped until it clung to my belt strap. I was hooked – literally! I tried to quickly catch the sweat that fell from my nose, but it was no use. It dripped on to Affa's hand. She would notice. It was only a matter of time.

Think fast, Yusuf. THINK FAST! I grabbed one of Affa's old scarves as bait and dangled it next to my pocket, teasing it. Come on come on come on. If Affa didn't bite, she'd pull me out of the wardrobe like a jack-in-the-box then hang me herself.

"Yusuf."

Dead. That was me. I was dead. Dead. Man. Dead.

"I worry about him the most. He's just..."

Oh, she was still talking to Khala. Phew!

I dangled the scarf closer to her fingertips and tickled them. She let go of my pocket and tugged at the scarf, pulling it towards her, but instead of closing the door, SHE FLUNG IT WIDE OPEN! I was exposed, completely exposed. The fresh air slapped my face and Affa's back only just blocked me from Khala's view.

DO. NOT. BREATHE.

DO. NOT. BREATHE. AT. ALL.

And just as Affa turned around to face me, she slammed the door shut, leaving me in darkness unseen.

THANK YOU, GOD. I knew You'd have my back! BOO-YAH! Agent Khan would live to see another day.

"He's just so young and so naive. The kid has no idea what's going on in the world." Affa continued.

Hold up one minute. I do too know what's going on in the world. I know that the ice caps are melting and that tigers are becoming extinct and that plastic is ruining everything. I know how stars are born and how big the galaxy can be and how small we are. I know loads of science. Does Affa even know that? Does she, does she, does she?

"He'll be okay. He's a bright lad." You tell her, Khala. You set her straight. "This is all beyond your control." Rewind, Khala. Rewind. But she didn't. "Trust that God has better plans. Leave it all to Him. That's what faith is, right?" The bed creaked again. "And don't forget that we're here for them too. Me and Aadam, we'll always be close by, won't we?"

If Khala only knew how close we all really were!

CHAPTER FORTY-EIGHT

"That was close, too close," I said to the mirror that night. My glasses were wonky and my hair had turned into ready-for-bed-hair already. It was time for Agent Khan to call it in.

Affa had gone to drop Aadam and Khala off at home so the house was quiet. Before she left, me and Aadam hid the henna cones under my bed and made a pact to never enter Affa's room like that ever again. It was just too risky. We could have really lost our lives out there. It was true what they said: a good spy knew how to escape, but a great spy knew how to survive – even if it meant putting his badge away.

TAP-TAP.

Amma opened the door. She looked like she was a thousand years old, almost as old as Nanu. Her cheeks were all bulldog saggy and her eyebrows had gone so low that they looked like they had given up on their jobs altogether. She plonked herself on my bed and rubbed her eyes with her scarf.

"You okay, baba?" Amma asked, patting the space beside her.

"Yeah." I sat next to her. Had she discovered our great henna cone plot? But how could she have known? We had been in tip-top stealth mode. Or MAYBE she had just chopped one too many onions. It was hard to tell sometimes.

"You sure you're okay, baba?" She licked her thumb, suddenly grabbing my face into a headlock, and rubbed my forehead squeaky clean.

"Gross, Amma." I freed myself from her strong arms and gasped for air. "I just had a bath!" She looked at me so carefully that I had to double check her soul was still here. "Are you okay, Amma?" Until that very millisecond, I didn't know that words could feel like bricks being shoved into your throat and planked into your stomach, but that was how it felt. Exactly how it felt.

Amma didn't answer. She just sat there, and this time stared into the mirror.

"I think you need a hug."

What? It was HUGS LAW. When mans needed a hug, mans got a hug. No questions asked. Look it up.

Amma's nose got all snotty and warm splashes of it slipped onto my neck. I wanted to wipe it off, but I didn't want to touch it. I didn't like her like this either. Not one little bit. Nobody, absolutely nobody (except me) makes Amma snotty like that.

"I don't want her to go either, baba."

That tight feeling in my chest was back again. Amma peeled herself off me and patted my eyes dry. Hold up, WHEN DID THEY GET WET? Amma must have transferred some of her eye juice to me. That was the only reasonable explanation. But wait, something was wrong. My eyes were leaking. Why were they leaking? How did I turn it off? Where was the switch? Why couldn't I find it?

What was happening to me?!

"It'll just be us soon, won't it?" Amma stuffed her scarf inside her nose and blew hard like a baby elephant. "Just you and me."

She let out a great big sigh and closed the door on her way out, leaving me alone.

WHAT!? NOBODY TOLD ME THAT NANU WAS MOVING TO MANCHESTER WITH AFFA.

It made sense… after all, Affa did EVERYTHING for Nanu. But NO WAY am I letting that happen. Over my dead zombie body.

NO ONE, AND I MEAN NO ONE, TAKES MY NANU AWAY FROM ME!

CHAPTER FORTY-NINE

When the summer holidays first started, I didn't know how to be the 'man-of-the-house'. But if watching our Affa-of-the-house had taught me anything (which she hadn't), it was that a 'man-of-the-house' looked after his own peoples. And if Nanu and Amma weren't my peoples, then who actually was? Except for Aadam - he was my peoples too.

I gathered my supplies quickly. Time was already running out. It wouldn't be long before Affa came back. I had 16 minutes 58 seconds max. Aadam and Khala didn't live too far away so I had to act fast. Unless Khala was showing Affa her garden, then she probably wouldn't be back full stop. (Khala

REALLY loves her garden.)

It was now or never.

Two cones would be enough. I was sure of it. Dropping them into my pockets, I listened out for the little click of Amma's bedroom door.

When I was two million percent sure that Amma was tucked away in bed (I couldn't take any chances), I rolled out of my room and slid quickly into Affa's like a ghost.

And there it was: the sleeping beast itself. It stood against the tower door, swaying dangerously.

For this to work, I somehow needed to get it on the floor. I poked it hard, expecting the hanger to wobble, but one of the little golden stones actually BIT me! It bit me! It did more damage to me than I did to it.

This was not going to be easy.

I had no choice but to yank it off, but I'd need something to cushion the blow otherwise Amma would sniff me out in a heartbeat. Piling all of Affa's pillows below it, her fancy cream blanket, and then the fluffy rug on top of it all would be enough. I was sure of it.

When the fortress of plumpness was ready, it was time to take on the beast. I needed something to protect my hands. I couldn't risk being snapped at again, especially now that I needed all my health points. But what could I use? What could I use?

The only armour in this battlezone was Affa's slipper socks. It would have to do. I slipped my hands inside the purple snakes and sniffed deeply. Gross! They definitely hadn't been washed in at least seven years. Yuk! I stuffed my hand in my mouth to stop myself from being sick - AHHHHHHHHH! I just tasted the sock. I JUST TASTED THE SOCK! Thank God it tasted like cheesy Wotsits otherwise I would have been a goner. Maybe I should lick it for good luck. No, no. That wouldn't be right. We didn't believe in luck.

Focus, Yusuf. Focus. After three, all I had to do was grab the dress and pull. That was it. That was all. As long and Nanu and Amma heard nothing, I'd be safe. Safe, safe, safe.

Okay, breathe.

Three…

(It would all be fine, right?)

I took a deeper breath. *Two…*

(They'll thank me for this, just you watch.)

One…

YANK!

Uh oh. **GULP.**

The space shuttle came tumbling down to Earth.

"Houston, we have a problem," I just about mumbled, gasping. The whole thing transformed into a giant octopus, attacking me from all sides. "Air," I breathed, trying not to drown in the fishing nets inside. But it was getting too much. The weight of it was too heavy and everything was getting dark. Even the socks had slipped away from me – traitors.

I was suffocating. I couldn't breathe! AFFA'S DRESS WAS TRYING TO KILL ME! Where was the light? FOR THE LOVE OF GOD, WHERE WAS THE LIGHT?

WAIT! I see the light!

"For my peoples," I gasped, dragging myself towards it with all the strength I could muster. I waded through the red sea, fighting against the strongest currents. "You can do it, Yusuf. You can do it!"

Finally, after a bazillion light years of slicing through the thrashing waves, my head broke through the surface and I could finally breathe again.

CHAPTER FIFTY

CREAK, CREAK, CREAK!

"What was that?" I whispered, trying not to choke on Affa's dress. The stones felt heavy on my teeth so I wriggled my tongue to get rid of it.

There it was again.

CREAK, CREAK, CREAK!

If I hadn't been two million percent sure that Amma was asleep, then I would have said that it sounded exactly, and I mean EXACTLY, like she was COMING UP THE STAIRS!

CREAK, CREAK, CREA—

Holy snot-pockets! CODE RED! CODE RED! CODE RED! AMMA was climbing up the stairs!

What do I do?

Just as my spidey-senses tingled, the door-handle moved. Quickly, I took a DEEEEEEEEEEEEEEEP breath and plunged nose-last into the red sea once again.

Time slowed to a stop and my heart drop-kicked itself. Maybe I really was underwater.

"Yusuf Ali Khan," Amma growled.

UNDERWATER GULP!

"That boy really is his Abbu's son." Amma ALWAYS says this like it's a bad thing.

Thank YOU, God! THANK. YOOOUUU. SOOOOOOOOOOO. MUCH! I could add human chameleon to my list of superpowers too.

But wait, hold up, why on the whole of planet Earth, the sun, the stars and the galaxies beyond did Amma always automatically think that I did it? I mean, she wasn't wrong, but she didn't KNOW that. Where was the sense in that? Nanu was just downstairs. It could have just as easily have been her. But NOOOOOOOOOOOO! Here I am trying to protect MY family and be the man-of-the-house and Amma just accuses me of— Wait, hang on, why did she sound SO CLOSE!?

"I better get this back up before she comes," Amma said.

UH OH. She would see me and then she would SQUASH me. The end of the world was near. But there was so much I hadn't done yet. I wouldn't ever have my own mobile phone. I'd never see Year 6. I'd never have my school jumper signed. I'd never even get the chance to grow!

I clung onto the dress for dear life. Maybe I could use it as a shield.

There was a LOUD SHUFFLE and I dug my nails in harder – toenails too – clinging to the poofy fishing net for dear life.

Amma grunted, her bear-like arms trapping me tightly into the chainmail. "I don't remember her dress being THIS HEAVY!"

She patted and yanked at the dress in frustration. Luckily, the fishnet absorbed the shock of her blows and I was just about able to turtle myself deeper inside for safety.

HOLY MOLY! Suddenly, a black dagger hanger almost pierced my eyeballs and blinded me for life. Like I didn't have eye problems already! Thank God for my quick reflexes. Batboy never went down without a fight. Did Amma seriously have NO EYE-dea that her ONLY SON was inside this dress?

I clung to the dress even tighter as it rose into the air. This rocket had blasted off and I was set to be the first human ever to fly into space in a dress (into Affa's space anyway). THIS IS SO COOOOOOOOL! Just wait until I tell Aadam!

But first, I had to make sure that the sweat that was sliding down my fingers didn't make me slip and fall to my death. Come on, Amma. Come on! I wouldn't be able to hold on much longer!

Amma groaned, slamming the hook of the hanger onto the door. She swung the dress so much that she was making me dizzy. If she didn't hook it up soon, I'd be sick on her peeping toes. "Something is definitely not quite right here."

CHAPTER FIFTY-ONE

Dear God,

I've made a lot of mistakes (and I mean a LOT). But Amma always says that You are the most merciful. I still don't really know what that means, but I will ask Sheikh Google later. All I'm asking is that YOU save me right now. That's it. That's all. JUST SAVE ME RIGHT NOW, PLEASE? An extra pretty please with a gulab jamun on top.

I was still too scared to open my eyes, but I wouldn't be able to hold on much longer. My fingers would fall off. It was hot and stuffy. I would probably die by being gassed by my own smelly breath. I was a gazillion per cent sure of it.

But wait.

What was that sound?

No.

It couldn't be.

Could it?

It almost sounded like… like… silence.

I peered over the top of Affa's dress and ducked back down again, my sticky hair sliding on the stones.

If my eyeballs hadn't deceived me, then I'd have to believe that Amma had just disappeared. POOF! Just like that.

Clenching my eyes shut, I listened closely. But there it was again. Silence.

A **PLOP! PLOP!** broke through the silence.

Was Amma returning? Was she on to me and my devious plan? Maybe she stood just outside the bedroom door, waiting for me to slither out of the dress so she could POUNCE.

I peeked just below my toes.

PHEW! False alarm: it was just the henna cones.

They must have slipped out of my pockets and rolled towards the fortress of plumpness.

I slipped out of the dress and slid quietly on to the floor. That was SO CLOSE. This whole thing was definitely a sign – a NEON warning sign – that said that this plan was absolute PANTS. It was time to abandon this ship and call it a night. It just wasn't worth it.

I patted the dress to remove any traces of me, and did a quick snoop around the crime scene to make sure everything was where it should be. Oh, of course, I'd have to disassemble the fortress of plumpness—

SQUELCH!

It all happened in slow motion like a fight scene from an action movie. My hands were invisible-chained to my sides as a brown gooey explosion burst from the henna cone I'd just stepped on and **SPLAT!** landed smack bang in the middle of Affa's not-so-sparkly wedding dress.

No. NO. NO. NO. NO.

THIS WAS NOT

HAPPENING!

I closed my eyes. Maybe it would go poof just like Amma had. COME ON. COME ON!

POOOOOOF already! GO POOF ALREADY!

But it didn't work. No matter how many times I opened and closed my eyes, it still didn't work. The poo, I mean paste, was still there. Affa would kill me. She would actually kill me. All those other times, I may have been a LITTLE dramatic, but this time she really would MURDER me and leave my rotting corpse as a warning for other foolish younger brothers. At this rate, Amma and Nanu would help her get away with it too!

Think, Yusuf. Think!

I'd have to wipe it off. I'd have to do it quickly before it sets. My brain was shouting, but my body wasn't listening.

JUST WIPE IT OFF! Wipe it all off. I could fix this. It wasn't too late.

Cold. The goo was really cold against my sweaty palms. I tried to clump up the paste in my fingers, but it wouldn't work. It just squished up more. Wiping it on my trousers, I tried again, pushing the poo paste to the side. BUT IT JUST MADE IT WORSE! WHY WAS IT GETTING

BIGGER? THIS DIDN'T MAKE SENSE!

There was a little splash on the floor. I WAS LEAKING AGAIN! In a panic, I reached up to wipe my eyes— OH NO! My face! IT BURNS! It burns!

And just then, at that very second, I froze. A jingle of keys tinkled downstairs and the front door clicked open.

"I'm home," Affa's voice shot up the stairs.

Ready or not, she was coming.

CHAPTER FIFTY-TWO

Don't panic.

Don't panic.

FOR THE LOVE OF NANU, DO NOT PANIC!

"I'm pooped." Affa's voice carried itself up the stairs as she flump-flumped her shoes off.

But then there was nothing.

Absolutely nothing.

Outside it was DEADLY silent.

But inside, my heart was punching itself, thumping my head, my ears and toes! It was going bonkers. My heart was on the loose!

Sabr, Yusuf Ali Khan! Patience. Beeeeeeeeeeeee patient ... like a pufferfish. Payyyyy-shence.

And pufferfish breathe out…

CRRRRRRRREEEEEEEEAAAAAAAAAAAAK...

RUN!

I ran across the room, slammed into the wall and

BOINGED straight back into the fortress of plumpness.

"Get off me!" I shrieked, untangling my foot from the quicksand below. "Come on, come on!."

Finally, my toes popped free and I fled to the one room where I'd be safe: the bathroom. It had a lock. But the bathroom sandals clawed at my feet and I tumbled face first on to the hard, bathroom floor. No time to be grossed out. I had to get clean!

Spinning the tap, I plunged my fingers into the sink, but the water shot everywhere. It smacked my glasses, almost blinding me, but the water didn't wash it away. The brown goo gushed down the sink, but the stain didn't move. I scrubbed harder. HARDER HARDER HARDER. But it was no use. There was no way to hide it. I had BLOOD (AKA brown henna paste AKA evidence) on my hands.

I turned the tap off and pressed my ear against the bathroom door. Locking it silently, I switched on my spidey senses and tried not to turn into jelly.

There was no sign of Affa. Zilch. Just the ticking timebomb that was the clock hanging in the hallway.

TICK-TOCK. TICK-TOCK. TICK-TOCK. TICK-TOCK.

Maybe Affa went POOF like Amma did. That could've happened, right?

My hopes were dashed when her cackle cut through the air like a knife.

"Who do you think taught her how to garden, eh?" That was Amma's voice!

Affa's pitstop bought me time. But how long would she stay for?

Breathe, Yusuf. Breathe.

If I had an asthma attack right now and had to go to hospital, Affa would forget about everything. She'd cry so much and pray for me to get better and the wedding would be called off and Nanu would stay too because there's no way she'd go to Manchester with me like that.

Change of plan: don't breathe, Yusuf. Don't breathe. But it was harder than it looked and my insides betrayed me. Every time I held my breath, it would just escape again. FOOLS!

I needed a back-up back-up plan. Scanning the room, I looked for a weapon. My only options were a toilet brush and a toothbrush (not mine), and I definitely didn't want to touch either of them. Maybe I could stay here forever instead. I could do it, I could. I had everything I needed to survive out here: a toilet, water, toilet water. Yeah. I'd do that. My bed could be the shower and maybe—

"I'm knackered." Affa yawned. "See you in the morning, in shaa Allah."

Nope. I'D BE DEAD.

DEAD. DEAD. DEAD.

I pressed my hands against my ears as Affa's door clicked open.

Then an earthquake **SCREAM** shook the entire galaxy.

GULP.

CHAPTER FIFTY-THREE

"I'M SORRY, I'M SORRY, I'M SORRY, I'M SORRY," I was yelling at the TOP of my lungs, but Affa kept banging the door. The handle rattled wildly. It wouldn't hold much longer! It was only a matter of time before it erupted. "NAAAANUUUUUUUUUUUUU!" I banged my fists on the door too. Somebody save me!

Where were the grown-ups? Why weren't they here? Why weren't they stopping this Hulk?

"YOU'VE RUINED EVERYTHING!" Affa bellowed. "You nasty little cockroach. You've ruined everything!"

The C-word, Affa actually said it, for real! Suddenly, there was an ALMIGHTY **CRASH** on the other side, making my shoulder tremble. SHE WAS TRYING TO BREAK THROUGH. I pushed harder against the door with all the strength I had left. **SMASH!**

"WAIT 'TIL I GET MY HANDS ON YOU, YUSUF ALI KHAN," she thrashed

against the door again. "Just watch!"

I pushed the handle up, but it was no use. My fingers were too slippy and they just melted off. "I didn't mean it! I didn't, I swear!"

"You," she pushed again, making the door quiver. "Little," and again, "LIAR!" and again!

"NO NO NO NO NO NO NO NO! You don't understand! Affa LISTEN!"

"No, YOU listen—"

Suddenly, everything … stopped. There was silence. This wasn't good. Not in a million years. THIS. WAS. NOT. GOOD..

"Eesoof Ali Khan," Nanu said quietly. "Open this door right now."

All the guts inside me plopped to my feet as Nanu tapped on the other side.

"Ammu?"

CHAPTER FIFTY-FOUR

Affa and Amma must have gone downstairs because by the time I was brave enough (and stupid enough) to open the door, it was just Nanu outside, gripping onto her walking stick. Her blue nightdress was covered in safety pins and crumpled at the bottom. She put a hand on her hip as her glasses slipped down to the end of her nose. Nanu pushed her spectacles back and let her eyebrows do the talking first. They were loud and clear: PRAY. TO. GOD.

"Come with me," she said after a long silence.

Slowly, Nanu opened Affa's door. She pushed it back and I followed her. Inside was a battlefield, a warzone, a… a… a graveyard.

"Look at what you did." Nanu said, pointing to the body of the dress. It lay on the carpet, its arms spread wide like a dying lobster. The white floor was covered in dried ~~blood~~ paste and brown goo covered all the sparkles of Affa's dress. The fortress of plumpness had rolled away and all that was left was the rug where the head of Affa's armour rested.

"I'm not even angry," Nanu said.

Don't say it. DON'T SAY IT! PLEASE NANU, DO NOT SAY IT!

"I'm just disappointed."

NOOOOOOOOOO!

Take it back! Take it back! Take it back! That was SOOO MUCH WORSE.

"We didn't raise you like this, beta," she said, wiping her forehead.

And THERE it was, the jalebi on the cake. Not Eesoof, not goru, but beta. Nice, sweet beta. I didn't deserve her.

"Clean it up. Now."

With that, and a swoop of her nightdress, Nanu walked out, leaving me alone with the corpse of Affa's wedding dress.

CHAPTER FIFTY-FIVE

It was past midnight and the whole house was asleep. With all the lights off and not a peep downstairs, I climbed into bed without bandages. Nobody would notice. Not tonight.

After Nanu left, I somehow managed to clean Affa's room before she tried to burst through the door again. Maybe Amma had locked her up and swallowed the key or asked Nanu to hide it inside her nightdress. But let me tell you that creeping around the habitat of a creature that wanted to kill you on sight was not easy. Not easy at all. Every time the clock ticked too loudly or the stairs almost creaked, my eyeballs nearly bulged out of their sockets and jumped pupil-first out the window. If it wasn't for my glasses, who knows where they'd be.

I pulled the blanket over my head and closed my eyes, so it was completely dark. Affa had never been this mad before – not even when I gave her a real-life fish-head lolly as an Eid present. She was so angry that day, I thought maybe her own head would explode.

But even after all that – after she tried to shove the fish particles down my throat, make me swallow its raw eyeballs clean off, and almost choke-slammed me to the floor – she still gave me a HUGE box of Jaffa cakes. All because that was the type of man-of-house Affa was. She was always thinking of everybody else and their Jaffa cakes. As Nanu said seventeen times, you just don't get people like that these days.

The hallway clock ticked louder and louder. The more I tried to block it out, the more it started to sound like claps of thunder. **TICK TICK TICK TICK TICKTICKTICK!**

"Stop it, already!" I hissed. "I get it! I get it, okay?"

There was no doubt about it, I had messed up BIG TIME. I didn't want to say it out loud, but I knew what I had to do. It was time to finally do what I should have done a LONG, LONG time ago.

With feeling-like-the-worst-omnivore-in-the-world mode activated, I crawled out of bed and pulled out the dusty prayer mat from behind the wardrobe.

I switched on the star-lights that definitely weren't nightlights, rolled the little mat out on to the floor and prayed. Dropping to my knees and raising my hands up in the air, I took a deep breath and started.

Dear God,

I know I haven't been the best brother in the world or even the best human being...

My fingers started shaking. A leaky splash of eye juice even splattered onto my arm and trickled down it. Soon, it was a whole waterfall.

Anyway, I know that I've done some things that I ~~maybe~~ shouldn't have done and said some things that I ~~maybe~~ shouldn't have said. But things haven't always been easy around here. Amma says You know everything ... so You MUST know how sorry I really am. I didn't mean for things to turn out like this, and now I think that maybe Affa won't talk to me ever again. So I just have three wishes left:

1. I won't ever do anything like this EVER again. Just please make everything better again.

2.   *Please tell Nanu, Amma and Affa not to kill me. I really like living with them and, apart from Aadam, I don't have anyone else.*

3.   *Please make Affa happy again and keep her happy always. That's all I want. That's all I ever want (most of the time).*

4.   *And just one more thing: please make sure that Affa still loves me. Ameen.*

I rolled the prayer mat away, turned off the nightlight and climbed back into bed.

I knew God always had a million things on His to-do list, but I really hoped that He was listening to me tonight.

CHAPTER FIFTY-SIX

TAP-TAP.

There were only three people who could be outside of my bedroom door: Nanu, Amma and Affa. I wasn't sure which one was worse.

I took a deep breath. I could do this… I was ready for it - as ready as I'd ever be (which wasn't really that ready when I gave it some extra thought). With no sleep and no plan of what to say or do, I hugged my pillow and listened closely for the next few words. They would determine my destiny.

The best case ending would be the Death Penalty. Affa mentioned it years and years ago. She said it was the worst punishment a person could face in this life. Going up against Death in a penalty shootout wouldn't be easy. He probably had years of practice while our school team actually chose a Year 3 kid over me in tryouts last year! (UPDATE: Affa has told me that the death penalty actually means. I like my idea better.)

The worst case ending would be packing my bags and going to Bangladesh for the rest of the summer ON MY OWN so I could learn some 'life lessons'. Rumour had it that the prisoners who were sent away never came back. MEGA **GULP.**

TAP-TAP.

Oh! I should have said something. Think fast, Yusuf! Think faster! Something polite, short, kind, not too much and not too little. Something that meant 'PLEASE DON'T KILL ME' in the nicest way possible and 'I'M STILL YOUR LOVING BABA' at the exact same time.

TAP-TAP.

Erm...erm...SAY SOMETHING! ANYTHING!

Oh wait, I got it!

It was perfect!

Why didn't I think of it before?

I held tighter to my fingers and tried to make myself sound more confident.

Deep breath.

And again.

And once more.

I only had one shot to say it. I couldn't mess it up. It was too important.

I cleared my throat and sat up straight on the pillow.

One.

Two.

Three.

"He- hello?"

Oh, man! Too shaky. Maybe I should try again.

"Yusuf Ali Khan."

Too late.

"Downstairs. Now." Amma said it sternly from the other side of the door then her footsteps trailed away.

They would all be there.

In the kitchen.

Waiting.

To pounce.

CHAPTER FIFTY-SEVEN

The smell of sana biran filled the kitchen. It was like the fried onions, mixed spices and all the chickpeas were dancing together at an invisible party and having a great time without me. They were obviously boogying with the kisuri, which Amma had swirled into a bowl with the biran and placed in the middle of the table beside Nanu. We only ever had kisuri and sana at Ramadan or when someone was ill. It was a specialty for those two times only. Never in my entire living memory had anybody ever made it otherwise. There was only one answer for this: it had to be a trap.

I scanned the room for Affa, double checking she wasn't hiding in the oven or the fridge (or the rice bin, the storage room, under the cooker, in the spice cupboard, behind the washing machine, above the dryer and in the salad bowl). When the coast was clear, I took another step deeper into the depths of the kitchen.

"Eat," Amma said, pointing to the bowl of suspicious deliciousness. Her golden bangles jingled. Could it have been a warning?

With no choice but to sit down on the chair opposite Nanu, I dragged the bowl closer to me. It squeaked as it crossed the table. Nanu scrunched her eyebrows and sipped the fresh tea Amma had put in front of her.

Slowly, I picked up the spoon and took my first bite. It tasted like... like... like anything but poison. It tasted like the breakfast of Jannah here on Earth. I took another bite, checking venom hadn't been squirted in the middle where I wouldn't notice it. After careful inspection, I placed the next bite in my mouth again.

"Eat faster!" Nanu barked and I almost jumped out of my seat. She raised her teaspoon threateningly.

I nodded quickly, stuffing four spoonfuls inside my mouth and chewing as fast as I could. Some of the kisuri escaped out of my mouth and slipped back into the bowl. I readied myself for another four spoons, but the dam would burst if I wasn't careful.

I raised my spoon again, preparing myself, but suddenly a cough exploded out of my mouth.

SPLAT!

Where did that go? WHERE DID THAT GO?!

I raised my head slowly, praying.

PLEASE GOD, PLEASE! I AM BEGGING YOU!

I peeked out from the top of my spectacles and there it was - my breakfast - all over Nanu's squeaky clean glasses. She smushed her lips together and wiped her forehead. Somehow it had managed to crawl down her face too.

"Wait, Nanu. Let me help you!"

That was what the right thing to do – right? RIGHT? I needed to clean up my messes and be helpful. BE HELPFUL, YUSUF! BE HELPFUL RIGHT NOW!

I dove for the kitchen towel before she could, sending my breakfast bowl spinning across the table and straight into Nanu's hot tea, before tumbling onto her lap.

Too many things happened at once.

As I yelled "NANUUUUUUUUUUUUUUUU," Amma, like a superhero, flew in and swiped the teacup, swerving it from Nanu's exposed target to the floor below. Nanu, who was blinded by her now-dirty glasses and held down by the breakfast bowl, yelped and shot up faster than a meerkat sensing a lion. The poor little teacup, Nanu's favourite one-of-a-kind white IKEA gem, hit the floor with a shattering crash.

REST IN PEACE to the teacup. And soon, me.

CHAPTER FIFTY-EIGHT

After Amma had cleaned the floor, Nanu had cleaned her glasses and I had cleaned up my act, the three of us sat down on the table and waited. I definitely couldn't go first so it was left to Nanu, Amma and their fresh cups of teas to decide who would.

Both of them sipped from their cups slowly. Nanu's sometimes even wobbled because she wasn't used to drinking from something that wasn't her little teacup.

"Yusuf," Amma began finally, rubbing her eyes.

I couldn't even bring myself to answer her.

Here it comes. My heart was preparing for the Sports Day Olympics already. It was trying to BOLT out of my ribcage with every nanu-second that passed.

"Why did you do it, baba?" She spoke very softly like I was ill.

Maybe the kisuri and sana was for me. Maybe I really was ill. The more I thought about it, the more it actually felt like it. My skin was on fire! My eyes were always leaking and my throat, my throat felt like it was trapping me in! Why didn't I notice this before?

Amma looked at me dead in the eye. "Why did you do that to your affa?"

I was blank. All the words had run away from my brain and I felt really small again. Tiny.

"Eesoof," Nanu began. She put her teacup down and it tapped the kitchen table. "When your amma asks you a question, you answer it."

I nodded. "I didn't mean it, Nanu. Amma, I swear I didn't. You have to believe me. It's just that Affa said that she was leaving and the man-of-the-house was now me and then I Googled what the man-of-the-house-did and the list was endless, but I tried my best and I only had £87.21 saved up, and Nanu scared me and then - " then I told them everything. Every little thing that happened from the beginning right to the very end. With every word that spilled out of my mouth and every time Nanu and Amma tried to hide a smile, I felt better. A WHOLE LOT BETTER. Like AWESOME-BALLS MILES MORALES SPIDERMAN better. Why didn't I think of this before? This was a genius plan! WHY DID I WANT TO ATTACK THEM WITH HUGS RIGHT NOW? Somebody hold me back!

"So you were in the wedding dress?" Amma asked when I said 'The End'. "No wonder it was so heavy. When did you get so heavy?"

"It's all the chicken samosas," Nanu chirped in, waving her hands. "They're finally working. This one isn't heavy enough in my opinion." She snatched my arm and raised it in the air, poking my chickpea triceps. "There's not enough to love here - not at all. I can't cuddle flesh and bone at my age, can I? It's not good for me."

I laughed and wriggled away from Nanu. "Do we have any chicken samosas left?" BAD MOVE. BAD MOVE! ABORT! ABORT!

Amma folded her arms tightly and gave me another death-stare.

"Chicken samosas left for Affa because she's leaving soon?" Phew. Quick save!

"Nice try." She said it with a smile and a nose twitch. That was a good sign. "You know, Yusuf, you can't stop this wedding."

"I know." I just wish it hadn't taken me a whole summer to learn that.

"Umar is a good man and your affa is really happy. We have to let her move on, even if it means she's moving out. Does that make sense?"

I nodded.

"But Nanu, you'll be going too."

Nanu held my hand. Her fingers were like little-ickle twigs. "Everybody has to go one day, beta. Death is a part of life. As long as you pray for your Nanu, everything will be okay."

HOLD UP!

WAIT!

THIS WAS NOT HAPPENING! THIS WAS NOT HAPPENING!

"Nanu, noooooooooooooooooooooo. No no no no no!" I grabbed both of her hands and shook them wildly. "Nanu, you're dying?"

"Yes, beta. Every single day, with every season that passes, every moment that falls away and every— "

"NOBODY TOLD ME SHE WAS DYING!" I burst from my seat. How could Affa even plan a wedding when this was happening? Did she have no heart?

"Yusuf, calm down! Your Nanu isn't dying." Amma pulled me back onto the chair since digging my toenails into the kitchen floor didn't work.

"But she just said— "

"Eesoof, I'm not dying right this second. I just meant— "

"But you just said—"

"Enough!" Amma raised her voice, silencing us both. "Your affa's leaving and your Nanu is staying with us until death do us part. Okay?"

"Oh, you should have just said. "

"Anyway, just because your affa is leaving home, it doesn't mean this won't still be her home." Amma took another sip of tea. "She's done more than she should have had to for us and it's time she does something for herself."

"So, we're not losing her?"

"No, beta." Nanu shook her head. "Things will be different, but that's not a bad thing. Change is good."

"Our family's growing, Yusuf." Amma ruffled my hair. "We just have a lot more people to love. Okay, baba?"

I nodded. "I think we deserve a group hug now."

HUGS LAW. Look it up.

I held on to them both tightly, trying not to suffocate at the same time. They smelled like tea and gwa fan and home.

CHAPTER FIFTY-NINE

I just had one job to do. Just one (HUGE) job: say sorry to Affa.

Armed with a pack of Jaffas (only half-eaten), some kisuri and sana (minus three bites) and a chicken samosa (okay, the crumbs), I marched straight to Affa's door. It was time to suit up into Batboy mode one final time. The plan was foolproof. I'd knock gently, say 'Affa-moni, pretty please may I come in?'. Then I'd look her in the eye with no fear just like a man-of-the-house would and say 'Please. I would like your forgiveness, please.'

I was as ready as I'd ever be.

I put the food down on the carpet and tried to silence the bees buzzing in my stomach.

"Shhhh!" I told them.

Ignoring the crashing in my ears and the thumping in my chest, I tapped gently on the door.

"Hello?" Affa quacked from inside.

CHANGE OF PLAN: there was no way I could

do this. I zoomed straight into my room and leaned against the door, trying hard to keep my heart in its rightful place. What was I thinking? That place was a rattlesnakes' nest. If I walked right into that trap, there'd be no way I'd come back alive.

Affa squealed as the chink of a spoon scraped the bowl. "GROSS! My toes!"

Uh oh.

TAP-TAP.

Ignore it.

TAP-TAP.

It'd go away.

"Yusuf?"

"He's not here."

WHO SAID THAT? WHO ACTUALLY SAID THAT?

"Yusuf, I can hear you."

"No, you can't." Why does my mouth keep moving without my permission?!

"Just let me in, will you?" Affa wiggled the door handle. "I won't strangle you."

"Or drown me?" I had to make sure.

"Or drown you."

"Or throw me out the window?"

"Boy, if you don't open this door, being thrown out of the window will be the least of your worries."

"Let me think about it." Play it cool. Play it cool. Be like Yasin Bhaiyyah. Everybody liked him, didn't they? Be like 'Yo, safe, innit, forgiveness, yeah? Gets me.'

I'd be able to do this.

"OPEN THIS DOOR RIGHT NOW, YUSUF ALI KHAN, OR I'LL KILL YOU MYSELF!"

I pushed against the door tighter. "On one condition."

"WHAT?"

"You wudhu." I shouted, gripping onto the handle.

Wudhu-ing is when you splash water over yourself to make sure you're all calm and clean and ready for prayer. I definitely needed Affa to be more calm-mode and less kill-mode right now.

"You want what now?"

"Just wudhu, okay. You need to cool down. I want to speak to you - not Shaytaan, thank you. Can you go wash yourself in the sink? Please."

Affa let go of the handle on the other side. "You're going to be the death of me Yusuf Ali Khan, you know that?"

"Everybody has to go one day, Affa. Death is a part of life. As long as I pray for you, everything will be okay."

"ARGH!"

I spidey-sensed her move away and head to the bathroom.

See? I'm learning already.

CHAPTER SIXTY

TAP-TAP.

Take two.

I sat on the bed with my shades on, looking cool and powerful. I had no idea where the Hulk Smash Hands boxing gloves were so I wore my P.E. socks instead. Don't worry - they'd been washed.

"Come in, my little friend" I said in my most impressive spy-villain voice. I wiggled my finger because all villains wiggled their fingers.

The door swung open and Affa came in slowly. Her eyes were red and puffy and her pyjamas looked like they'd been soaked.

"I've got really bad hayfever," she said, picking her eyelashes. "It's just really bad lately." Her voice was thick and snotty.

Play it cool. Play it cool. Like 'Yo, safe, innit, forgiveness, yeah? Gets me.'

"I'M SO SORRY, AFFA! I didn't mean to be such a bad brother. I'm going to miss you so much and I don't want you to go!"

I slammed my fists on the floor (when did I fall to my knees?).

"Please forgive me. Please, please please. I'm begging you! I AM BEGGING YOU!"

"Whoa, whoa. Steady. Stop touching my toes."

"BUT THEY'RE FREAKISHLY LONG!" I cried, stroking the toe-thumb with the sock. "I'M GOING TO MISS THEM!"

When she couldn't drag me off her, she flopped to the floor, sitting cross legged, and pulled me up. "I forgive you, kiddo. You know I do, don't you? I always do."

Affa moved to the side so we could both lean back on the wardrobe.

"I don't think I can be a man-of-the-house. I can't be you, Affa." There. I said it. "Being a hero all the time is HARD."

She laughed and nudged my shoulder. "You know, not all heroes wear capes. They don't all have powers, Hulk Smash Hands or gadgets like that." She pointed at my socks.

"Yes, but I don't have any money either. How are we going to pay the bills or go on school trips or buy Jaffa cakes. I'm a growing boy. I need my vitamins."

"Don't worry. Yusuf, look." She nudged me again. "Being a man-of-the-house isn't about the money or the bills or things like that. It's about being here. Right here."

"On this exact spot?" What would I do when I needed a number one or number two?

"Duroh."

I'm not even sure what this means.
I don't think anybody does.

She shook her head and laughed. "Of course you can move, fool. It just means that you try to think about people other than yourself. Like just talk to Nanu - ask her how her day's been. Has she eaten? Ask Amma if she's okay, if she needs any help. She won't, but that's all it is.

248

It's not about doing everything. It's just about the effort. Does that make sense? Do for them what you want done for you."

I nodded. "Maybe I can leave my Batboy days behind me now. It was stressful."

"Just be Yusuf." Affa said, running her fingers through my hair. "Well, a kind and helpful, Yusuf. You gets me, bruh?"

"I gots you."

CHAPTER SIXTY-ONE

"So you didn't get a punishment?" Aadam asked, moving out the way for another Khala to pass. We were sitting on the sixth step up from the bottom. All the other floor space was taken and the whole house was squashed up for the Mehndi night. If all the windows in the house weren't open, we'd be tinned sardines.

"Amma said she's thinking of one," I said, flattening myself against the wall to let Rabia Affa through. Her eyebrows said she wasn't happy, and I didn't want to get in her way when she stormed down the stairs in her cactus sari. I had definitely learned my lesson the hard way. Boss women shouldn't be messed with. "I'm hoping she forgets."

"I told you it was a bad idea." He grabbed two samosas from a bowl that was being passed around and gave one to me.

"It was your idea!"

Nayma Affa gave the samosas back to us. She

was wearing a bright orange dress and looked a little bit like a jalebi.

A jalebi is a deep fried (DELICIOUS) orange sugar swirl dipped in syrup.

"Can you make sure Amina, Aneesah, Aisha, Samiyah, Shajeea, Sairah and the rest of them get one?" She called above the buzz. "Just pass it backwards. Leave one for Hidayah and Maryam too."

"Let's just hope she does forget, okay?" He turned to the trail of little people behind us. The nine of them were throwing balloons off each other and screaming. Kids these days. They were so childish. All they ever did was shout. I could barely hear my own thoughts.

"HEY, TINY PEEPS!" Aadam yelled at the top of his lungs, making me jump out of my skin. "TAKE YOUR SAMOSAS OR I'LL EAT THEM FOR YOU!"

They all froze and stared at the bowl hungrily.

This couldn't be good.

"Mine, mine, mine!" they began to chant like people possessed.

"Put the bowl on the top step quick!" I pushed Aadam forward. "Hurry! Before they eat you too!"

With only a second to spare, the bowl of spinning samosas made it to the feeding floor before the little beasts gobbled them all up.

"Phew," I said, staring at the crumbs they left behind. "That was close."

"Too close."

We tried to sit back on our step, but our spot had been taken.

"You snooze, you lose," Nazifa Affa said,

not once looking up from her phone. She put her earphones in under her scarf and pretended we didn't exist. Naz Affa, Khala and Khalu came from London this morning. They set off so early that Naz Affa was probably an expert at snoozing already. There was only one thing for it. We had no choice but to sit at her feet. Luckily, she didn't mind.

"So what's Affa going to wear now that her dress is all funky?" He tugged the collar on his kurta. School boy error: never get the collared ones. Even I knew that.

"She's wearing Amma's old wedding sari. There aren't as many gold nettles so it'll probably hurt less."

"Oh yeah," Aadam looked up. "I forgot your mum was married once."

"Yeah," I said, getting up to look for Affa. "Me too."

I didn't like lying.

CHAPTER SIXTY-TWO

It took AGES to find Affa in the maze of our house. I looked absolutely everywhere - twice! I even tried to count the amount of people squeezed inside these teenie-weenie walls, but every time I thought I'd finished counting a room, more people would come into it. It was useless. At this rate, the answer would be infinite.

DING-DONG!

Who used a doorbell at a Mehndi? I didn't know people still did that.

I opened it only to find a bright red Ms Hayley on the other side with a t-shirt that said 'WOKE'. She definitely looked too awake to me.

"You're back! Did you have a good holiday?" I asked, sniffing for Peagreen. Right now, a tiny shih tzu could cause a HUGE problem, especially if Aadam was around.

"Never mind my holiday!" she said, pointing her finger like a mad woman at Khalu and Rabia Affa's cars. "Are these yours?"

I followed her finger again. She was trying to air-stab the fourteen cars that had already swarmed into our street.

"Nope, sorry." I shook my head. Why would a 9 ¾ year old drive. Wasn't that against the law? She really was losing the plot.

"Of course they are!" She stomped on the spot three times. I kind of wanted to do it with her. "What do you mean they're not yours?"

"What do you mean 'what do I mean'? They're not mine, I promise." I tried to close the door, but she put her foot in the way.

"That's it!" She sounded like an angry teacher. "Let me talk to your dad. Bring him here!"

"He's not here, either," I nudged her feet away with the door. I had to do it three times before she even budged. "Okay, thank you. Come again."

Phew. Now where was I?

DING-DONG!

"Ms Hayley— Oh."

It wasn't her and her hot temper after all. It was another white lady with a sunshine yellow dress.

"They aren't my cars." I explained, waving her away.

"Sorry?" She looked around the street. "What cars?"

Before I could say another word, Tariq Bhai's voice boomed across the garden. "Oi, oi, lad. Alreet? You've grown, haven't you?" He fixed the hedgehog spikes of his hair and held his hand out for a fist bump as he made his way inside. "Where are my manners? This is your bhabi," he said, pointing at the sunshine dress. "I don't know if you heard that I got married a little while ago."

Heard? I didn't even get an invite to the wedding. Oh, I had heard about it, alright. Just like he would have heard my grumbling stomach.

"But … why are you white?" I asked Bhabi.

She burst out laughing and her blue eyes bounced with her.

"Yusuf, man. I've missed you." Tariq Bhai gave me a great big bear hug and almost squeezed the living daylights out of me. "Family come in all shapes, sizes and colours, bruv. Now where's this bride-to-be?"

At that very second, like Bhai's prayers were being answered, a big cheer came from the living room. The clapping in the house felt like thunder as Tariq Bhai led us into the room.

Affa was there, sitting on the floor, looking like a ripe lemon in her floaty dress. There was a HUGE, and I mean HUGE crispy fish on a metal tray in front of her.

Around it were spicy Bombay potatoes, fat juicy prawns, fish masala bites, swirly, twirly, whirly cucumber pieces and other bits of mouthwatering goodness.

"You look amazing," I said to the fish. It truly did. Truly. Is this what true love felt like?

"Awhhhh, Yusuf," Bhabi said, clapping so her bangles jingled. "Aren't you the cutest?"

"Nah, don't get too excited," Tariq Bhai said. "He's talking to the fish."

"What?" She didn't sound impressed.

"Come on," Affa said, patting the floor. "Let's tuck in, shall we?"

Rabia Affa, Nayma Affa, all the Khalas, our cousins, my new bhabi and the rest of us crowded round to feed Affa. There were so many fingers pulling at the fish that sometimes it was hard to tell which hands were mine. It was only when I wiggled my arm that I knew for real.

"Say bismillah, Yusuf," she said, stuffing a jumbo prawn-Bombay potato sandwich in my mouth.

I always say this before I eat anything. It means 'in the name of God'.

CHAPTER SIXTY-THREE

It was the dead of night and the curtains were tightly shut. The clock had already struck long past the hour of bedtime and Affa had transformed into a mad scientist. Her hair was all wild and frazzled, her cheeks burned red and she cackled very quietly like a deep-fried samosa. If we were any louder, we'd wake the eight other sleepers who were snoring away. Since Rabia Affa was one of them – and she was SUPER grumpy, even when she was awake – we didn't want to risk it.

The torchlight on Affa's phone fell face first onto the carpet with a thump. We froze, Affa stretching a bandage and me trying to stay balanced on one foot. The snoring had stopped so quickly. We couldn't tell if they had woken up or not. When the KHAR-SHOOO engine started up again, I let go of the breath I didn't even know I had held in and watched the shadows of Affa's fingers crawl towards her phone.

Phew.

"I'll miss this, you know." Affa whispered, wrapping me up mummy-style. She looked over my head to see if Nanu was still sleeping on the bed. After we all cleaned up, Nanu had tried to fight us all just so she could make her bed on the floor with everyone else. In the end, Nayma Affa and Nazifa Affa held her walking stick and gwa fan hostage, forcing her to take her own pillows with her.

"At least she won't shout at you anymore," I said. "You definitely won't miss that, will you?"

Affa giggled quietly. "I'll probably miss that the most. You know Nana was so chill. If he was still alive, he'd love all of this. Every single moment of it. I wish you'd met him."

"Me too." I lifted my arms so Affa could do my back properly.

"They were a proper team, you know. A force to be reckoned with. I miss him. He made her so happy even though they bickered all the time. Like Sherlock and Watson."

"And Wallace and Gromit?"

"Them too." Affa screwed on the lid of the cream and slipped it under the bed. "When she shouts, she's not really shouting. She just cares too much that's all. She's both a worrier and a warrior and she doesn't want us to end up like Amma was back in the day. Can you understand that?"

I nodded. "If anything, Nanu is and always will be the man-of-the-house."

Affa laughed again. "You're right, you know."

But then she suddenly stopped. Her eyes froze. I turned around – there was nothing there.

"Affa?" Something wasn't right.

She grabbed her neck quickly like someone was attacking her.

"Affa?" I squeaked.

"I… I… I TRUSTED YOU! I TRUSTED YOU!" she whisper-shouted. She flopped onto the floor with a flump and my laugh escaped my mouth before I could stop it.

THWACK!

"Who did that?!" I gasped, trying to recover from the almighty force of the pillow. I didn't even know humans could throw like that.

"Oi!" Rabia Affa shouted, Only Rabia Affa would shout about us waking everybody up by shouting and waking everyone in the room up. She held another pillow like it was Thor's hammer. "Bride-to-be or not, tomorrow's the big day. We need to sleep – and Yusuf! This is the girls' room!"

"But the boys' room smells like farts." I whined. My plan was to stake out here for the night unnoticed. "I can't breathe in there."

"I don't care. Take your inhaler with you," she threw another pillow at me. "I love you both, I truly do, but if I hear one more peep, I'm going to knock you both out."

"You already did," I mumbled, trying hard not to throw the pillow back at her.

She must have heard me because she said, "If you're done being bandaged, take it with you – the door is that way!"

And with that, I was banished. With the pillow in hand and nowhere else to turn, I made my bed on the stairs, praying no one would mistake me for toilet roll in the dark.

CHAPTER SIXTY-FOUR

Yusuf, what an excellent summer diary and what a journey you've had! Great work! I look forward to reading about your next adventure soon.

Miss Minchell

Five reward points

CHAPTER SIXTY-FIVE

Being in Affa's room without her this time was like being time-warped to a place that didn't really feel right. It was like I was an underwater spy searching for the world's most high-security treasure chest, and then finding out that inside it was just a Shaun the Sheep poster. I guess now that the wedding was over, I didn't really know what to do – at least not until school and mosque started up again and that was a WHOLE week away.

Amma and Nanu had gone to bed and Khala and Aadam had already said goodbye and told us they'd see us in the morning. So the whole house was quiet and empty and Affa's room was a silent cave. It would take me and Aadam about seven years to inspect all of its treasures.

I closed her curtains and lay down on the floor, pretending to be an astronaut that was floating in space. Affa once said that in space there was no gravity and there was nothing there to pull you down. She actually had a telescope in this mess somewhere.

It was still here, right?

I crawled towards the bed where all the things forgotten were. Stretching my hands underneath, I searched for the telescope.

"It has to be here somewhere."

I stretched and stretched, but all I found was a CAPTAIN AMERICA box!

No way! What was this doing here?

There was a little white tag on the side that read 'For the man-of-the-house'.

That couldn't be Nanu, could it? Why would it have Captain America on it if it was Nanu's?

I carefully lifted the lid. If it was Nanu's, I could sellotape it back together at least.

Inside it was a little blank notebook covered with zombies and mummies. Not just any zombies and mummies, but MEGA ZOMBIES AND MUMMIES! It HAD to be mine. (And even if it wasn't, I called it.)

I opened it up and on the first page was a picture of me, Affa, Nanu and Amma.

Underneath, it read:

'I noticed you writing all summer, Yusuf. This is for your next great adventure...

Love always, Affa.'

266

ACKNOWLEDGEMENTS

One of the most beautiful things about Yusuf's tale is that when you open up these pages and fall into his words, you get a tiny glimpse of my world – and I mean my whole world because this book is a tribute to my family. It's filled with so much love, so many memories and so much hope. This is us and everything we stand for – know that we are blessed.

To my parents who gave us a place to call home, I am so grateful for your guidance, your love and your unwavering faith in the woman I've become, even when I've lacked it in myself. To my sister, Smeagol, for being such a big part of this. Jazakallahu khairan for combing through every single line of Yusuf's life – twice. A little thank you to Mina too – she's definitely Yusuf's cousin in some other life. To my brother and my bhabi for being there, always – with food, afternoon tea parties, and takeaways at the ready.

A whole lot of love to my uncles and aunties who make up every branch of our family tree. It's because of you guys that we have so much love. I pray that our kids are blessed with what you gave us. To my siblings by extension, my 'cuzzys', and where my heart lies – to every single one of you, may He always keep us close. May we continue to be a source of strength for each other and, as time passes, may we continue to find home in our love for one another. And to dadhu, the bedrock of our family ties and the inspiration for Nanu – you always kept us close.

To the real Yusuf and Aadam, and for my nieces and nephews on both sides of my family tree, I hope you see yourselves in here and know that you have so much love around you. Don't ever forget that.

To my agent, Polly Nolan, thank you for making Yusuf possible when you did. It was when I needed him most. I just didn't know it then. To my editor, Eishar Brar, this was my dream project, the story I didn't even know I had in me, and I don't even have the words to explain how much this whole thing has meant. Representation matters so much and it's an honour to be a part of the Knights Of team – a million thank yous and a whole lot of love for understanding this without question, and knowing how important it was to share this with the world. To Naz Abdillahi for helping me shape this into something more meaningful and a thank you to Farah Khandaker and Marssaié for bringing this story to life.

To Sophie Minchell, as always, for everything and more.

And lastly to Abdul, for being my home away from home.

BURHANA ISLAM

Author

Born in Bangladesh, raised in Newcastle and currently residing in the outskirts of Manchester, Burhana Islam is a storyteller who is passionate about exploring themes of heritage, belonging, identity and faith in her work. She studied English Literature at Newcastle University before deciding to become a secondary school teacher, sharing her love for stories with a new generation of curious, young minds. MAYHEM MISSION is her debut children's fiction book, and she is also the author of AMAZING MUSLIMS WHO CHANGED THE WORLD (Puffin, 2020).

FARAH KHANDAKER

Illustrator

Farah Khandaker is an illustrator and designer currently based in Dhaka, Bangladesh. She received her masters with distinction from Nottingham Trent University specialising in Illustration. She's worked across children's books, logos and editorial. Her work is fun and engaging with vibrant colour schemes and unique characters.

KNIGHTS OF is a publisher focused on actively finding voices from under-represented backgrounds. They are committed to publishing inclusive, commercial books and ensuring that the most diverse team possible, from across backgrounds and communities, work on every book. #BooksMadeBetter